MANIAC

BOY

GAME

OVER

"David Goudreault stays his course, explaining nothing, forcing the reader to make up his own mind about this character, lost and endearing in spite of his madness, his self-absorption, and his cruelty."
—*Culturebox* **(France)**

PRAISE FOR *MAMA'S BOY BEHIND BARS*:

"Another essential work for anyone who wants to clearly see the things our society would rather keep hidden, the things that so clearly reveal who we are."
—*info-culture.biz*

"*Mama's Boy Behind Bars* is, without question, even better than *Mama's Boy*: delicious observations, hard-hitting humour, a majestic style, and a sense of rhythm that will make many more experienced authors envious."
—*Huffington Post Québec*

MAMA'S BOY GAME OVER

Book*hug Press
Toronto, 2020
Literature in Translation Series

FIRST ENGLISH EDITION

Published originally under the title *Abattre la bête* © 2017,
Les Éditions Internationales Alain Stanké, Montreal, Canada
English translation © 2020 by J.C. Sutcliffe

The production of this book was made possible through the generous assistance of the Canada Council for the Arts and the Ontario Arts Council. Book*hug also acknowledges the support of the Government of Canada through the Canada Book Fund and the Government of Ontario through the Ontario Book Publishing Tax Credit and the Ontario Book Fund.

We acknowledge the financial support of the Government of Canada through the National Translation Program for Book Publishing, an initiative of the *Roadmap for Canada's Official Languages 2013-2018: Education, Immigration, Communities*, for our translation activities.

Book*hug Press acknowledges that the land on which we operate is the traditional territory of many nations, including the Mississaugas of the Credit, the Anishnabeg, the Chippewa, the Haudenosaunee and the Wendat peoples. We recognize the enduring presence of many diverse First Nations, Inuit and Métis peoples and are grateful for the opportunity to meet and work on this territory.

Library and Archives Canada Cataloguing in Publication

Title: Mama's boy, game over / David Goudreault ; translated by JC Sutcliffe.
Other titles: Abattre la bête. English
Names: Goudreault, David, author. | Sutcliffe, J. C., translator.
Series: Literature in translation series.
Description: First English edition. | Series statement: Literature in translation series

Translation of: Abattre la bête.
Identifiers: Canadiana (print) 20200357905 | Canadiana (ebook) 20200357964
ISBN 9781771666176 (softcover) | ISBN 9781771666183 (EPUB)
ISBN 9781771666190 (PDF) | ISBN 9781771666206 (Kindle)
Classification: LCC PS8613.O825 A6213 2020 | DDC C843/.6—dc23

PRINTED IN CANADA

The safest refuge is a mother's breast.
Jean-Pierre Claris de Florian, 1792

To Randall P. McMurphy, my man

PROLOGUE

At the end of this story I'm going to kill myself. And then die. That's just the way it is. All good things must come to an end, including me.

You shouldn't even be holding these pages. The only reason you're reading my words at all is thanks to providence, or some other occult miracle. You cannot comprehend how lucky you are. Unless you have faith. God is everywhere, and I am here; I'll let you draw your own conclusions.

In all modesty, I'm just a man, a mortal. Already dead, in fact. But people with great destinies tread this earth, a race of men who don't just mark history but write their own. I am one of this species too majestic to be demolished or sink into the mud of common insignificance. Like a conqueror, a literary genius, or some graffiti celebrating Mark and Nicole's love on a blasted-out rock at the side of the highway, I will leave a trace.

Others will come after me. The most wretched will merely imitate me; the most noble will be inspired by my works. But I won't be here any longer. These are my last words: read them in memory of me.

It's all over. The story begins.

1

OPTIMISM

Craziness isn't a mental illness, it's a sign of intelligence. I'm batshit crazy. With a batshit crazy hard-on too, which makes the nurses uncomfortable. Right now, three nurses and some massive security dude are trying to attach me to the restraint bed. I'm bare, butt-naked, greased with margarine from head to toe, flailing around like an epileptic fish in a rowboat. Getting my day's exercise. Fling my weenie here, bang my head there, and bingo, I manage to bite the fat little nurse's thumb. There's shouting and threats, and blows flying every which way. I'm having so much fun!

Occasions for enjoyment are rare at the Philippe Pinel University Institute of Legal Psychiatry. Deprived of alcohol, drugs, and porn, we fall back on meds and violence. Humans are naturally creative, and I'm very human. I'd collected all my Seroquel tablets over the previous week and ground them up on the sill of the barred window in my cell. I watched Montreal bathing in its smog, I promised myself I'd wreak havoc out there one day, and I sniffed the whole lot up my nose in a single snort. *Raaaah!* There's no denying that the pharmaceutical industry makes excellent psychotropic drugs. I needed to act fast before

I collapsed or fell into toxic psychosis. If it interacted with those intravenous tranquilizers they had me on there might be some nasty surprises in store.

I'd caused this ruckus in my cell by way of introducing myself. I demanded to see the psychologist, promised to calm down as soon as I was allowed to talk to her, pleaded that she alone could soothe me. And then I stripped and buttered my body, exhilarated. It was exciting, in the erectile meaning of the word. One last grand gesture before my final departure.

With a kick at the red-headed nurse's mouth (she wasn't even sexy) and an elbow in Godzilla's stomach, I had the upper hand again. *Bof, bam, thwack!* I like to add in a soundtrack when I fight. I was out of control. *Whack!* I even managed to grab the female intern by her hair. *I've got you, you ugly bitch!* Nothing personal.

The misbehaviour management specialist had fallen into my trap. I'd been sweet-talking her for nearly a year, asking for her advice, faking anxiety attacks, validating her role as a helper, while deep down she was about as much use to me as a panful of bacon to a vegan. Suspecting nothing, she demanded access to my cell and started heading down the hallway before she'd even so much as looked at what was happening in my dungeon. Epic fail! As soon as I heard the latch sliding, I pushed open the door and thrust my tumescence at her. *Well, hello!* Total joygasm: her intern was with her—a beautiful plump brunette who was overendowed in the mammary department. And *bam*: in three steps I was flattening the student to the ground and gripping one of her breasts in both hands. Just to torment her.

This is the bitch of an intern whose ponytail I'm holding right now. Her compassionate smile gave way to a grimace of hatred. She hadn't stopped mooing since I groped her on the corridor floor. Sometimes she begged for help, sometimes she exhorted someone to kill me. Her screams drowned mine out, but I held tight to her mane of hair with both hands and didn't let go. Mike Tyson in the security guard's uniform forced me to let go with a swift right hook to the nose. It's been broken so often; I keep hoping that one day a well-aimed blow will set it straight again.

In the meantime, I blocked the charge of the badly paid moron who was preventing my escape from the solitary confinement cell. The sweating nurses were finally managing to strap me down. I fought back, but they succeeded in tying down my legs while Hulk Hogan overpowered me with a mix of jabs and uppercuts. The intern carried on providing the scene's soundtrack, presenting with one of the first symptoms of acute stress and soon-to-be PTSD. *Aaaaaaagh! Aaaagh!* Her supervisor was trying to calm her down, reassuring her that it should never have happened, that it wasn't her fault. While I collected my wits, the three uniformed bitches managed to tighten the leather strap around my left arm.

I like constraints, both in sex and in literature. They make you more creative, arouse your imagination. But you have to know when to stop, to respect people's comfort zones. And nobody was respecting anything here now, those chicks were yanking on the restraints with all their strength while my B-list Muhammad Ali carried on hammering away at my face with his knuckles. He didn't even need to—I was already tied up like a string of sausages. He would pay for this one day; even Ivan wouldn't seem especially terrible compared with my vengeance. Crack! One final right hook to my temple. The show was nearly over, my hard-on was fading.

Then Demontigny, another giant from the security team, showed up in the doorway, out of breath. *Too late, you cunt!* Even so, counting the psychologist, the intern, the nurses, and the security guy, I'd mobilized seven employees in one fell swoop. If I hadn't been firmly cinched to the bed, I'd have been strutting around with pride in my ability to unify the civil service.

Before Ginger closed the door, I noticed her gaze lingering on my prominent muscles, which gleamed with vegetable oil. Despite the blood flowing down my face, I flashed her my most beaming smile and a wink. Women are sensitive to the non-verbal language of virile men in a vulnerable situation. It's well-documented.

The noise of the metallic locks rang out, the light went out, and once again I was plunged into darkness in myself. Cut off from the world.

If you're going to be alone, you might as well be in isolation.

Following Little Miss Piaf's example, je ne regrettais rien, absolutely nothing. Not the weeks of stealth it had taken me to gather up all those little packets of margarine, nor the relatively consensual caressing of the intern, nor the epic battle and the multiple bruises that came along with it. The end justifies the means, especially when you're taking on the big guys. I no longer had anything to lose except for a couple dozen books; they force-feed us pretty well at Pinel.

This period of confinement was going to allow me to set in motion Operation Final Jerk-Off. I'd spent too long vegetating; all my senses were going numb in these sterile corridors. But it would soon be over. I'd mobilized every scrap of lucidity to fine-tune my escape plan. My furry tongue could already taste the sweet brioche of freedom, my return to civilian life, and the first step in my reunion with Mama: jailbreak time!

Any day now I'm going to be with Mama again. She doesn't know it yet, but she's going to have something to be very happy about. It's crazy how much we're going to love on each other, sitting around in pyjamas sipping our marshmallow-smothered hot chocolates as we tell each other our life stories, snuggled up together on a super-expensive big leather sofa that I'll have bought for her despite her kindly protestations: *No, son, you shouldn't spend so much money on me, I don't deserve all this love and loyalty you're showing me when I couldn't help being an absent mother*... I will comfort her with a long kiss on her old, wrinkled, single-parent forehead and then let her continue ...*but now I'm going to spend every minute of my life with you, my protector of whom I'm so proud, because you are handsome, generous, and so intelligent. Thank god you finally escaped and you found me again to shower me with the warm devotion that all mothers, all over the planet and ever since the dawn of time, have dreamed of*...

And I would clasp her to my heart, and she would spill a little now not-so-hot chocolate on my pyjamas and we'd burst out laughing together, our eyes sparkling as our family blossomed. How sweet dreaming is when the dream is readying itself to break reality's chrysalis.

But dreaming is a muscle that can get tired. Hours were ticking by, the Seroquel euphoria was slowly fading, and I was starting to nod off. I desperately tried to fantasize about my outside life, but I was having trouble inside. I'm too smart to let myself daydream too long. With all my strength, I hung on to positive thoughts and the strength of will, but my mind was focused on the tribunal, mired in resentment, and still fixated on the witnesses at my last trial. Lubricated by all my held-back tears, hatred and pain mated in my wounded soul.

My weaselly lawyer had argued for a trial in front of a judge and jury even before the charges against me had been laid. He assured me I needed to plead insanity, that I was an ideal case. I didn't let his compliments go to my head, but I just wasn't convinced he was right. Rumours were rife at Donnacona Prison, some of my fellow inmates even claimed that Pinel was worse than jail; they actually injected us with prison bars there instead of locking us behind them. The most alarmist even went as far as saying things were better in jail, where you just had to put up with some animal messing with your ass instead of a psychiatrist messing with your head. But if these allegations came from the most dishonest criminals in the country, could I trust them? Ratface, looking neckless in his gown, said no. The expert opinion of those nutbars wasn't worth anything, I'd be treated better in a psychiatric hospital than in a prison, and murdering Butterfly and my so-called sexual assault could be the keys that opened the door to a better life. Every cloud has a silver lining. Without flinching, the old charlatan promised me that the detention conditions would be less severe, that it would be easier to get released, that I'd have access to a bigger library. I could keep books and dictionaries in my room. *Even anatomy textbooks?*

Even anatomy textbooks! He'd found my soft spot, although I'm not as sensitive as I look.

I was resistant: a trial in front of a jury would mean more media coverage of the whole thing. I was afraid people would lie about me, tarnishing my image, or that Mama would stumble across a newspaper article and believe the whole violent-rape story. I can justify the murder, but violent rape isn't quite so socially acceptable. And those bastard prosecutors upheld that I was a "dangerous pervert," even though "rejected suitor" would have been a way fairer description. I felt as though they were preparing me to be torn apart on the stand, that they would totally wreck my image. But old ratface assured me that, quite the opposite, the trial would be my chance to defend myself and—the deciding argument—to see Edith again. It didn't take any more than the prospect of laying eyes on Edith for me to get back in the saddle, brandish my noble knight errant's fist, and charge ahead. No precipice could stop me.

The preparations for the hearings had turned out to be unbearable. My lawyer was trying to get me to say the unsayable, wanting to put words in my mouth. I told him to get lost, but he came back stronger: *At a minimum, you have to admit you mistreated her, you misread the cues or something…*

With the back of my hand, I waved at him to shut his big mouth. *Love isn't a landing strip, you don't have to wave flags. You just feel it inside, you know? And I felt it so strongly. You can't even imagine.*

He pointed out that he had four children with his childhood sweetheart, but I interrupted him, it was irrelevant.

Love is easier to make than to talk about. And we made love and talked about love at the same time, imagine that! Nobody can take that away from us, it's just mine and Edith's.

In spite of my lyrical flight worthy of Molière in his good period, the lawyer just hammered his same theme over and over again: *In court, like everywhere else, it's not the truth that counts, but what you can make people believe.* Recognizing the limits of his competence, he suspected he would be unable to make people believe that Edith had consented, the circumstances were pretty damning. But if we went with the judge-and-jury option, he could fudge things and sell them the idea that I was even crazier than I really am. Then they would have to care for me instead of locking me up.

I had to admit, the old wheeler-dealer had a point. I suggested he get himself a more Anglo-sounding pseudonym so he'd be accepted by his bar colleagues. He sighed and asked if I was anti-Semitic. I replied, almost sincerely, that I have nothing against Jews. I do admit there were some geniuses in the family tree: the guy that invented the bagel, for example, and whoever wrote *The Diary of Anne Frank*. That was a bestseller, they should totally do a sequel. Maybe even a trilogy.

Underneath his exasperation, he believed in my chances of being judged not criminally responsible. Despite my previous convictions, he kept banging on about how I was the most innocent man he knew. Right from the very start, he'd worked to dress up my image. He bought me shirts and a new pair of pants, with zero concern for my testicular comfort: I have a very delicate scrotum. Even though I told him I was hip-hop in my soul and my style was a way of expressing myself, he wouldn't drop it. I had to dress appropriately and keep my pants crotch in the right place. At the same time, he pressured them to get my teeth fixed, to improve both my pronunciation and my credibility. That was pretty sick: with my new white grillz I could rap away or give talks without any speech impediments.

Edith was luminous, practically phosphorescent. In the shadows of the court I had eyes only for her. Pregnancy made her more beautiful. On the first day of the trial, I'd noticed her increased bust size. She'd gone from barely appreciable breasts to pretty respectable boobs. Nothing to upset me there. And I could get my fill of staring at them without worrying about getting caught, since Edith was avoiding looking at me.

I was kind of in denial, trying to believe that she just felt awkward seeing me again, eight months after our last meeting. I could even have attributed this lack of civility to shame, since she hadn't written me a single letter all the time we'd been apart. But after the third day of the trial, after she took the witness stand, I had to face the facts: she didn't love me anymore. Women are more volatile than the perfume they wear. Some seducer must have taken my place and messed with her head. Or some fucking community organization of hysterical feminists must have brainwashed her so she would fit their statistics better.

She denied everything about us: it was as if there was nothing left of our great love, as if all our plans for the future had been entirely imaginary. There had never been any ambiguity, she had never led me to believe she could help me or my accomplices escape, she had never consented to a sexual relationship with me.

Liar! I heard you come!

Listening to the judge's vociferations as he threatened to expel me, Edith burst into tears. She was playing this brilliantly. What a cruel innocent.

The judge allowed her a break. I was sure my lawyer was going to seize the opportunity to yell at me. I was surprised to see that he was pleased about my interruption. *It really highlights the level of cognitive distortion we're dealing with here. Don't hesitate to say whatever else you think of.* He would later regret that advice.

Under cross-examination, Edith admitted she was carrying my child. Clearly she was a manipulative bitch but not an unfaithful whore. When my lawyer expressed his astonishment that she would keep the product of what she herself called rape, Edith retorted that her conscience and her moral rectitude forced her to protect this child, and abortion was totally against her values.

This child, she said, not *this girl*. My son was clearly a boy! Given the flood of testosterone pulsing through my body, it wasn't surprising that I was only capable of producing a kid with balls, but I was still moved. And proud too: from a genetic standpoint, this was a great success, the ultimate achievement—reproduction. I shed a quiet tear and asked her what we should name him. The judge sighed and ordered my lawyer to control my impropriety. My lawyer tutted and winked. I hoped Edith would agree to call him Kaeven, Tommy, or Steven.

But right now she wouldn't even say my name. Or look at me. It was a far cry from the days when she used to tell me I could trust her, that she'd be there for me if things went badly. Women are like luck, you always think you deserve them, but whenever you really need them they abandon you.

Things were getting pretty emotional. The last key witness: my "mother." My mother who wasn't really my mother at the end of the day, as the Scots say. With circumstantial proof, cross-checks with social services, and geographical incompatibilities, there was no possible room for doubt: the lady who I used to spy on in Sherbrooke could not be my mother, certainly not my birth mother. You can always find good reasons for being wrong, but I'm humble and I recognize that I was mistaken. It happens to everyone, it's well-documented.

And this poor, insignificant, childless woman had come to snivel in front of the judge so she could relieve her distress and express her *trauma at being stalked and harassed by a murderer.*

She was overdoing it a bit; I had to step in. *This is a court-room, madame, not a therapy group!*

As per usual, the judge pulled me up for impertinence while encouraging the crybaby to wallow in pity.

I was sinking into self-pity myself when I thought of all that time I'd wasted on a stranger. But since I was a real phoenix prone to compulsive reincarnation, I could see hope being reborn. If this woman wasn't my mother, all the rejection I'd suffered at her hands was nothing to me. My real mother was waiting for me out there somewhere, and I knew she would be happy to welcome me with open arms.

The trial was dragging on. Since I was a defendant who'd been transferred from another prison, my detention conditions were appalling. They wouldn't even let me renew my stock of books, so I had to keep going through Poe, Kafka, and Lautréamont on a loop, which was driving me crazy. I was eager to get settled down permanently, whether with crooks or crazies. I aspired to stability. But my lawyer was extremely thorough, demanding additional expertise, adding witnesses to shine a light on my childhood, which was both disturbed and disturbing, my life in care homes and the whole nine disasters. I'd had an assful of his processes: I was ready for things to end badly as long as they would just end.

To motivate me, he reminded me how important it would be if we could kill two doves with one stone: if we won this trial and I got sent to Pinel, we had a good chance of getting the Butterfly murder charges dropped. We had to gamble everything on my mental alienation. And pray to St. Jude, patron saint of dudes with nooses around their necks. To be sure of the outcome, he encouraged me to interject whenever I felt like it. That would spice things up a bit and bolster his case.

Your Honour, you're a big sucker!

After that second of silence that froze the courtroom, everyone heard my lawyer sighing *Nooooooo…*

I made the most of everyone's surprise to give the judge another slap-down: *If justice is an apple, you're the worm eating away at it from the inside, Your Honour. I would argue that—*

My lawyer threw himself at me, grabbed me by the shoulders, and begged me to shut my trap. It was the first time I'd seen him turn purple. Against the white collar livening up his ridiculous robe, it actually kind of suited him.

Judge Belkorchia, who seemed more suspect than ever, started banging on his mahogany desk to restore order. With an exemplary air of false professionalism, he advised the jury to not let themselves be influenced by my outbursts and to concentrate on the lawyers' defence speeches, on my criminal history, particularly the second-degree murder, and on his own recommendations. And then he picked right back up where I'd interrupted him, right in the middle of defining "aggravated sexual assault."

I really liked the idea that I'd been armed when I was making love to Edith, but it was purely circumstantial: I had a helicopter to reroute and a mafia boss to get out of prison. Sure, I'd slightly mutilated Edith's face and fractured her jaw before I deflowered her, but there again you had to put it into perspective: I was stressed to the max.

Persnickety to a fault, the judge decreed that the fact I'd given her herpes constituted an aggravating circumstance. In my opinion, you don't share those intimate details in the early stages of a relationship. And it would be seriously out of place in an exciting hostage-taking situation.

It's not like I could get my hands on any rubbers, asshole! Ya think I shoulda wrapped my dick up in an old Skittles bag?

That was one step too far for the decrepit old asshole. The guards took me out of the courtroom so he could finish corrupting the jury in peace. What a jerk. He claimed to be expressing himself in the name of the law, but he was totally disrespecting my right to express myself. I had just enough time to wish aggressive testicular cancer on him before I was dragged with dignity out of the courtroom.

I wouldn't get out of this scot-free. Our justice system does indeed work, and it works particularly well for police officers, lawyers, and judges. All the talk about criminals committing crimes with impunity is just for show, even the most light-fingered Mafioso ends up meeting the long arm of the law. In any case, all we were playing for was the decision about which cage I'd be locked away in. Either I'd be heading back to prison with the dangerous crazies or I'd be going to Pinel with the dangerous crazies. Not exactly a fun betting game. It was like Kurt Cobain making long-term investments—nobody was going to get a whole lot of interest.

I didn't understand what I was winning, but we won. My lawyer was ecstatic, as happy as a mohel brandishing a bleeding foreskin. He'd won with his criminal irresponsibility, my mental alienation. Forever after, I was now officially crazy.

Even if we'd won a victory over the judge's crass rudeness, I regretted the judgment. For me, it didn't change anything anyway: prison or hospital, I'd escape either way. But Edith was crying and raging in her mother's arms. It tore me apart from my guts to my heart. Her refusal to even look at me once during the trial hurt me, of course, but I still loved her. Even if it was unfair to accuse me of assault when all I'd done was love her, I'd have happily accepted a conviction if it would have made her happy. That's right, I'd have been willing to get life imprisonment to make her feel better, if she wanted me to be guilty so badly. Despite the lie she was wrapping around herself, I'd done it all for her. The more I thought about it, the more I wanted to cry myself, so overwhelmed was I by my generosity of spirit.

After half a decade here, I can tell you that a psychiatric unit is like a prison, it just gets disinfected more often. They play around with the terminology so they can get particular grants, but basically it's the same thing. The hole is called *the room reserved for isolation*, the cell is what they call *our bedroom*, handcuffs are known as *medication*, and detention is called *therapy*, but make no mistake about it, it's the same psychological violence, the very worst kind: man being imprisoned by man.

When you're tied to the restraint bed, feet and hands strapped to the four corners of the metal frame, you have to give up a lot of things. For example, scratching yourself, practising onanism, and physical exercise too. Your movements are hobbled; the only thing you can do is wiggle your toes and wave your hands. But that's all I needed. My palms managed to reach the pointy corners of the metal frame. I rubbed away on the right angles, then rubbed them some more, until my hands bled.

Bee-yatch, bee-yatch, bee-yatch. I could hear my psychiatrist's high heels getting closer to the isolation room. Audible from over a kilometre away, they clacked their echoing rhythm in the corridor. *Bee-yatch, bee-yatch, bee—* Here she was. From behind the padded door, I recognized her exaggerated Italian intonation even though I couldn't make out her words. The blinding neon lights clicking on reminded me I'd been rotting in isolation for an eternity and a half. I clenched my fists, and blood trickled over my wrist. The din of the locks gave way to the squeaking of the door, which gave way to the security guy, who gave way to the psychiatrist.

Dr. Milani. A tall, beautiful blondie bedecked with a doctorate and a certain way of carrying herself that made her seem as self-important as a twentieth-century escort girl. She really thought she was somebody. But the sad thing about people who think they're somebody is that the somebody is actually less interesting than who they might be otherwise.

Important detail: she was a lesbian. Well, I didn't know that for sure, but she'd resisted all my advances and had short hair. With her salary, which was pretty damn near as high as a man's, the old battle-axe could trot out the most disagreeable attitudes. The tabloid editorial writers were right: women had emasculated the stronger sex and killed all hope of social balance, economic development, and masculine thriving in North America.

I was calm, aggressive, and peaceful, relaxed like the string of a bow, ready to welcome her. She stood at the end of the bed with her Cerberus sidekick and scrutinized me from head to toe, with an obvious pause at my crotch. Nobody had even bothered to dress me. She scribbled a few things in her black notebook— or maybe she was making a quick sketch of my penis—before she even deigned to say a grudging hello. She was the queen of bitches. I would have crowned her with a shrimp ring, but seafood is expensive even when it's on sale. She didn't deserve them that much. I had to be happy with treating her like a high-class prostitute, imitating her accent just to show her that her Italian—and probable Mafia—connections didn't scare me at all.

She tapped her temple with the tip of her index finger— whether to remind me to think or to imagine shooting a bullet at me, I couldn't say. *So, looks like-a you went on a crrrazy rrram-page today? I should have known it, it's been a while since-a you blew yourrr top. I'm going to have to incrrrease your intrrravenous sedatives, unless you can give me an explanation?*

I needed to get rid of her as quickly as possible, before she could see I was self-harming and start suspecting I'd put Operation Final Jerk-Off into practice.

No, I have no explanation or excuse, I just wanted to touch that little cunt's big boobies. You must know, Doctor, Lacan's proof that it is sometimes impossible to tie a knot in your dick to strangle your desires.

She stayed stoic, but I'd hit the bull's eye, I was disturbing her and she was going to get out of there as fast as she could. Women stick together when it comes to men. It's so sweet the way they unite to wave pink ribbons or denounce their rejected suitors.

That's a prrrretty weak arrrgument, I know you usually have more to say. She moved nearer to the bed, the only piece of furniture in the room, screwed to the floor, the epicentre of this room devoted to problem cases. *You'rrre a prrroblem case, you know, I've been following you forrr five yearrrs and I still don't know wherrrre we'rrre going... I'm perrrplexed.*

She narrowed her eyes slightly, pondering like a philosopher or a Japanese zen monk. Zen my ass, I can't think of anyone more stressed than a Japanese person. She took another step closer, to right about the level of my penis, which wasn't looking its best under the cruel fluorescent lighting. The guy moved nearer too, but she raised her hand to show him she wasn't afraid of anything and he should stay back.

I encouraged him too. *Good dog, stay!*

She leaned over my face, just a few degrees, before murmuring for my ears only, *You arrren't a monsterrr, you'rrre a human, and humans can be currred.* I would have shot a gob of spit right in her ugly mug if I hadn't had a lump in my throat blocking the way. I swallowed the whole lot and closed my eyes, to sulk and to put an end to the conversation. I wasn't going to let myself slip on the muddy terrain of emotions.

She could whisper aphorisms and prognoses at me until she was blue in the face, she was still a massive bitch and I was still going to escape and never come back. With all her book-learning, she ought to know it's harder to mend a broken heart than to fix a heart attack.

Here's a space-time paradox for you: we have to follow the line of time, but all our clocks are round. The Italian she-wolf had given me a strong dose of sedatives and tranquilizers, plunging the needle into the depths of my thigh—which is, I must confess, slightly chubby—maybe four or nine or twelve hours ago. Go figure! It felt pretty good at the time and it relaxed me, but now the buzz was fading. *For rrreasons of trrreatment, not punishment*, she was letting me stew in the isolation cell for a full day in addition to the night I'd already served. I guessed I must be about halfway through my punishment, more or less, and I was bored shitless in between fits of rage. Tying down a man who's reacting against his imprisonment is about as logical as giving a machine gun to a psychopath who's having an epileptic fit. It could have nasty consequences.

They untied me so I could eat, under supervision, and loosened the restraints to clean the leather bed when I soiled myself. Seconds became minutes, minutes became hours, and the hours stretched out endlessly, as boring as a white girl's ass.

I wasn't exactly having the time of my life in there—and even Patrick Swayze died in the end. I was bored to death. Fuck, I'd already wasted five years in this crazy asylum. Without writing or loving, which means without living. My son would be going to school soon. And my mother wasn't getting any younger either.

Apart from escaping and finding Mama, I didn't really have any other plans for my life—I barely even had a plan for staying alive. I was floating in a pond of ambivalence. One part of me hoped I'd die this year, at twenty-seven, like all the good ones: Kurt, Jim, Janis, Amy, a few hundred rappers, and other geniuses of my calibre. I was afraid of getting to thirty. As every teenager knows, thirty's old, forty's dead. Beyond that, it's all just futile, dogged endurance, old-people obstinacy. Decrepitude and cellular degeneration get going in your mid-twenties. Creams don't do anything. When the elasticity and plasticity of your skin—and even your hair pigment—desert you, you poor fucker, it's because your body's perfect genetic programming is sounding the death knell. The time allocated to you to seduce, conquer, screw, and reproduce is coming to an end. Death isn't an end point but a process; the start of death comes long before the end of life. Those old hags who get themselves sliced and diced and then patched back together are right: nothing is more valuable than youth. After that, it's dereliction, death, or retirement.

You have to look things in the face, even when they're turning their back on you. *Tempus fugit* too fast, in Latin and in English. Yes, time flies, and I need to think about flying too. My recent escape attempts had all been total fiascos, but even Jesus fell down three times on his way to Calvary and he didn't let it stop him from reaching his goal. This time I'll do it right. And if necessary, I'm ready to die in the attempt. Anyway, you have to hope for a violent death, very violent. That's the only way to avoid suffering, aging, and illness. If it's unexpected, so much the better: a violent death that sneaks up on you, with no degeneration and no waiting. Death is always suffering, but a little less so when it's sudden. That's something I wish for everyone.

I twisted my wrists as hard as I could, I stretched the straps as far as they could go, and started up with the palm mutilation again. The hemoglobin was flowing, I was rubbing and gouging away, intoxicated by my desire to escape and by the smell of blood.

As a modern-day adventurer, I don't take risks anymore, the risks take me. I'm a wild mustang, encapsulating the best of man, as long as the man is straight. And you can certainly take that as a given.

2

PIETY

What we call reality is just one option among many, and it's rarely the best one. Everything's relative, even Einstein. From a metaphysical perspective, Einstein never even existed. Every lie is a truth in waiting. And depending on the point of view you adopt, there's always a way to present things in a favourable light. Even if it turns out to be a blinding light.

Did you really meet Jesus? Simon was amazed by my story.

I didn't just meet him, he penetrated me. And I closed my eyes to add a little ceremony to my words.

Simon was hopping from one foot to the other in excitement. *Can I see them again?*

I glanced furtively around to check that no nurses or security guards were watching us and I opened my hands to his astonished stare.

Oh my God, your stigmata!

If faith can move mountains, surely a believer could get me out of Pinel. I'd been working on this guy for six months, eating his desserts and preparing my escape. Simon, my five-foot-two psychotic Christian, blond and gentle as a sacrificial lamb, embodied the ideal tool to extricate me from the high-security claws of our psychiatric prison.

Apparently we can't all be good at everything. On the other hand, it certainly is possible to not be good at anything. That's how it was with Simon, and he'd developed some incredible religious beliefs to help him deal with being a loser. From a human perspective, religion is reassuring: all men are equal, redemption, dignity of the soul, etc., etc. He'd been shooting up the Bible for too long. Whether it was little Jesus, his Virgin mother, or their pet angels, this devoted idiot hallucinated a halo on anything that moved.

Unfortunately for his sister, he also saw Satan from time to time. And he'd recognized him in his younger sister's features. He didn't take the risk of playing exorcist, he simply got rid of her head. As a matter of fact, they're still looking for it.

I have nothing against sectarian or religious convictions, especially when they might be useful to me. Personally, I think every time you get down on your knees you move farther away from heaven, but I believe in respecting other people's beliefs, even the stupidest ones. But the psychiatric team didn't share this opinion. Poor old Simon had been subjected to massive doses of tranquilizers since he'd arrived, interspersed with targeted electrocutions. And it was all in vain: nothing could stop the members of Christ's inner circle from visiting him.

Is there a saint among us, Simon?

Nervous glance over his shoulder. He wriggled a bit. *Ooh, yes, archangel Jeremiel is with us…*

Of course he is. *Ask him if my stigmata are the final sign we've been waiting for.*

Simon started muttering and raising his eyes to heaven,

smiling into space. *No, the divine entity says it's not the sign.*

What an asshole! *Yes he did, I heard him too, he said it's the sign, ask him again and you'll see.* You should never underestimate the power of suggestion on any psychotic worthy of the name.

He started mumbling again. Silence. *Oh, you're right, it is the sign!*

Hallucinations are like old electronics, sometimes they need a helping kick before they'll work. *The stigmata don't lie, Simon. Today's the day we put things into action!*

A summer Monday morning, troops on the ground reduced, great weather, docile mentally ill guy under my thumb: all the elements were in place. And after my little weekend crisis, the staff would definitely be thinking I'd stay relaxed for a while. After the rain the sun? No, no, no. After the rain the thunderstorm, you bunch of fuckers!

There are no stupid jobs, but there are professional assholes. You find a particularly high concentration of them in the field of health and social services. To my great sorrow, I've always been well-placed to know this.

I'd chosen the best day to give Simon one last little twist of manipulation and then escape. The very young, overly nice nurse, Marie-Chanelle, posed no danger. She was a chubby hippie addicted to meditating. She didn't need any medication, she was constantly floating in the clouds with no intention of coming down. Kindly and a little pretentious, she loved leading art workshops, fingerpainting, and other such nonsense that was supposed to help sick people get better. Marie-Chanelle also did animal therapy with some patients, but I wasn't allowed to take part. Too bad for the animals. I had a lot of love to give them.

The most obedient patients recited mantras with

Marie-Chanelle. I felt attacked by her gentleness. She probably wore an organic linen G-string underneath that immaculate uniform. I'd still have fucked her though, she had a nice smile. Maybe I'll meet her again on the outside.

As well as a nurse, there were two giants in charge of keeping order in our section, because it was supposed to be pretty dangerous. But it really wasn't. Our prescription meds were so strong and incapacitating that they took away our desire, if not our ability, to assault and rape each other. In fact, they defused all possible desires. The chemical straitjackets they made us wear in the form of pills and shots ensured the institution stayed mostly peaceful, but now and again some specimens—like me—indulged in a flash of lucidity, a low-key crisis, or an assault.

In one corner of the common room, Jamal was looking relaxed as he flicked through an adult colouring book. He was a lazy dude and liked to keep his distance from actual work. Except when it was something he enjoyed, like the time he fractured my wrist in a three-against-one attack. He was violent and arrogant—the perfect security guard. He was on my revenge list, but revenge would be a dish best served once my trail had gone cold. He was a champion idiot, Jamal, a show moron. It would only take the tiniest brush of a wing.

In the office, the real target of the manoeuvre, Big Marcel, was watching over the ten or so crazies all busy puttering around or drooling on themselves. I had to get into this inaccessible office to neutralize the electronic systems, get my hands on the keys, and force the mechanical locks to obey my will. I'd spent so many hours spying on the agents as they tapped in the code, tracking their habits and figuring out the ideal parameters for Operation Final Jerk-Off. They could virtue signal all they wanted about their patient care, about how they prized cure above coercion and other pompous paradigms, but except for its sterilized corridors and white coats, this section of Pinel was still a prison—and, as Casanova noted before me, *prisons are always more beautiful from the outside.*

But I could never hit Marcel, Simon whined.

When you're dealing with mentally ill people at this level, they're like athletes, they need a lot of hand-holding. *But it's not Marcel, you know that, Simon. What's his name?* My puppet was turning out to be trickier to manipulate than I'd expected. *Go on, say it, what's his name?*

Marcel Demontigny.

Exactly. Demon-tigny. He's not human, Simon, he's one of Satan's soldiers, a foot soldier from the eighth circle of hell. I've told you a hundred times. And what's your name, Simon?

Bishop. His voice quavered.

Simon Bishop. And only the bishop can conquer the demon, right? At that moment I opened my palms right in his face, exposing the holy proof of my divine connection.

Alright, if you say so.

Simon headed for the office without even needing me to remind him of the plan's steps. Haloed in his usual serenity, he was sporting the same half-charming, half-lunatic smile he'd had plastered on ever since he'd arrived at the hospital. He banged on the armoured door. No patient was allowed to be within two metres of that door, and there was a red line on the floor to reinforce it. But Simon could go and knock on it without raising the tiniest suspicion. And Marcel took the bait.

Marcel was a Pisces ascendant brute and a security veteran. He'd been an enforcer in warehouses and bars and he'd come to finish up his career with the crazy cuckoos and mindless idiots at Pinel. He'd seen—and assaulted—it all before, this Marcel. He was in his late forties and fit. Superfit. He trained hard and shot up protein shakes non-stop. His skull didn't match his thickset body: right where you would have expected to find a bulldog head, there was actually a long, emaciated face. Despite his efforts to be stylish, he was a morphological disaster. He clearly didn't get laid much. Proud right to the roots of his sparse, jet-black-dyed hair, he groomed his fancy beard just to come and guard the numbest mentally ill people in the metropolis.

Marcel didn't seem quite so cocky with Simon in his arms, doggedly gnawing at his forehead and gouging his face. He'd opened the door to find out what sweet little Simon could possibly want, only to hear Simon suddenly yell, *Deeeeemon*, jump at his throat, and knock him to the ground. Simon, the absolute incarnation of furious lunacy, was hitting, scratching, and biting, and Marcel seemed unable to defend himself. Poor dude wasn't managing to protect his precious face very well. Guess our guard wasn't as strong as he looked. Bodybuilding is more about appearances than strength. It's just bulking up with makeup and air around the bones: bodybuilders are basically just sluts.

Jamal, the other guard, was more predictable than Donald Trump on Twitter. He was frozen in position, totally paralyzed. A few morons were huddling on the chairs or whimpering, terrified of either my ally's grunting or the victim's pleading. The ones who weren't quite so high emerged from their torpor and exhorted Simon to even greater violence. Marie-Chanelle, mesmerized and too far from the door to escape without having to go past Simon, took shelter under a table, emitting some rather erotic noises despite her distress. It was the perfect surprise effect. As

I hoped, Operation Final Jerk-Off was jisming right in their faces, and they were getting an absolute mouthful.

Before Jamal could figure out what was happening under his very eyes, I ran over to him and swung my fist at his teeth. Occupational hazard. It was an excellent right hook. Scarlet gushes spurted out, splattering everywhere, a firework display of spraying blood. Even for someone of an ecumenical bent like myself, it was beautiful to see. The nurse and the lobotomy gang made me feel so proud with their *ooohs* and *aaaahs*.

Carried by my own momentum, I hit the floor with Jamal. He wanted to grab his radio, his alarm button, a weapon, anything. In spite of the force of my punch, I hadn't managed to KO him. Knocking someone out is more difficult than cartoons would have us believe. Too bad, I was going to have to kill him. I'd foreseen this circumstance and was carrying a rope made from underwear elastic. Just in case.

To the horrified shouts of some psychotics gathered in the corner of the room, and to the applause of another group of less sensitive fellow inmates, I got Jamal with his face on the ground. I rained a shower of blows down on him, punched him between the shoulder blades, slipped my rope around his neck, and strangled him. He struggled as much as he could, but I was stronger. I tightened the cord with all my strength, bashed his head on the floor, squeezed hard, and, after a short but interminable moment, Allah called Jamal to him. I quickly tied a bow around his neck as a nice finishing touch.

Ali Baba's cave had opened for me at last; Simon had proved to be the Open Sesame I'd been hoping for. Under his attack, an idiot-savant mix of punches, head butts, and bites, Marcel had been neutralized. I raced into the office, leapt over the bodies tangled on the floor, and grabbed the bunch of keys. Finally I had the keys to Pinel in my hands! I tapped in the six -digit code that deactivated the alarm and hammered the switch with my fist. I had yearned so much for this switch! For the last few years it had been my constant desire. The electronic door control, the inviolable Cerberus of our section, was powerless. And there was light! The green bulb was shining over that fucking door through which I could normally walk only under escort. My fantasy was coming to life before my very eyes. Freedom was calling out my name. I was coming to her, coming inside her, I was ejaculating with happiness inside myself.

Anything could happen, and everything did happen. In spite of Marcel's screams of pain, I noticed the agitation ramping up in the main room. Awesome! A handful of my stooges, drunk on all the action, were getting ready to start a riot. It was just a little riot since there were only five of them to raise a ruckus. A sixth was devoting himself to caressing Jamal's body and dribbling. The seven other patients in the section and the nurse had crept off to panic in the most tucked-away corner of the communal space. There was shouting, crying, and sighing, and it was all stressing me out more than necessary. *Come on, Simon, let's get out of here!*

He lifted his head calmly. His mouth and chin were covered in Marcel's blood, *amen*. Leaving the poor bleeding bodybuilder to exsanguinate in the fetal position, Simon fell into step behind me and we came out into the communal room, which cranked the tension up another three notches.

I couldn't believe it when I saw Jamal regain consciousness, rip off his garotte, and call feebly for help in a muffled voice. Killing someone is more difficult than it looks in the movies. A recently arrived young father-killer started trying out Jamal's head as a trampoline, thereby relieving me of a tedious job. With a bit of luck, we'd get out of there without setting off the main alarm. To keep my morale up, I whispered, *I'm going to see my freedom and my mother.*

Behind me, I heard Simon say, in the same tone, *I'm going to see Jesus and your mother.* Worrying!

I'd scored the hat trick: group homes, prison, psychiatric hospital. It's all the same old same old. One group of pretty fucked-up humans getting to be in charge of another group of other pretty fucked-up humans. They're just not healthy places. I needed to get out of them once and for all and suckle some emancipation from the teat of liberation. I needed to do this whatever it cost, and I was prepared to make them pay whatever the price.

With Simon on my heels, I ran across the corridor like a ninja, which is basically running on tiptoes while stopping yourself from moving too fast. It sounds complicated but it's effective. We'd gone through the security doors of two sections without attracting any attention. I used Marcel's precious keys to unlock the last door on the floor and felt my luck turn along with the deadbolt. Finally I was regaining some confidence and some control of the situation; it's not just masturbators who can get a grip on themselves.

Just as we were about to take the stairs down to the ground floor, I heard a mooing from the end of the corridor.

Wait for me, guys! It was fat old Lavallée, not caring about his knees, chasing after us heedless of our ninja tradition. *Wait for me, I'm coming!*

Behind him, the apprentice rioters were advancing as they brandished chair rungs, table legs, or shit.

Noticing my annoyance, Simon asked me if I wanted him to bite fat Lavallée in the face to make him leave us alone. *That won't be necessary. Run!* We gobbled up the steps four at a time. We made it to the bottom just at the moment the main alarm began blaring. Its strident noise tore our eardrums. I pushed open the door from the stairwell and came face to face with Milani, my stuck-up madam of a psychiatrist. There was no time to lose, I planted a kiss on her mouth. With tongue. Then I threw her to the ground. *Ciao, Isabella Rossellini.* And off I sprinted.

Nursing staff were swarming the corridors, slowing me down. I pushed one against the wall, flattened a security guard, and finally arrived outside, breathless, my lungs searing. The seconds were ticking away.

They must have been kinda busy with the mutiny on the second floor, because the way ahead was free and clear—just as I would be very soon. As I was running, I kept pondering how to deal with the two guards at the entrance, how to get them out of their little guard station to neutralize them, and then get me inside it to open the main gate.

Was it little Simon's presence bringing me luck, forcing fate's hand? Simon's god certainly hadn't bothered to help us. We were nearing the entrance, I could see the guard hut waiting for us with its door wide open. The two guards we'd been worried about were busy defending themselves against Lavallée, who was totally out of control, rolling his blubber on first one and then the other, punching wildly in all directions. Where had he come from? It's a riddle wrapped in a mystery wrapped in a giga-enigma. All the better for me though, since he was keeping the final line of defence occupied. The three men on the ground were so caught up in their exchange of blows that they didn't even notice me when I lowered the handle that controlled the doors. A ray of sunlight beamed into the shadows of modern psychiatry. Simon slipped through, and I followed immediately after. Like William Wallace, Nelson Mandela, or a pet bird, I shouted, *Freedom!* as I crossed the threshold of my cage.

I was finally leaving that screwed-up institution behind me, but Simon still clung to my ass. I had to get rid of him as soon as possible. But I couldn't reveal this part of my plan to him. We all have our secret garden, even if it's just for burying the bodies. I had to act quickly. The police sirens were getting closer; we were more likely to be spotted if we stayed together. And I had to keep in mind that he was a dangerous mental case. There was no guarantee I might not suddenly look like a good martyr to him. He was trotting after me on Boulevard Henri-Bourassa. I stopped short just as he caught up with me, and then I pushed him in front of a car. *Bang!*

But the old granny behind the wheel still had good reflexes and stomped on the brakes of her little red Echo. Instead of running over Simon and killing him there and then, as I had calculated, she just gave him a good whack. His head shattered the windshield before he leapt back onto the tarmac and lay inert a metre away from the vehicle. The grey-haired good Samaritan jumped out of her car to help him. This really was my lucky day!

As I revved the Echo's engine, I glanced in the rear-view mirror. I saw Simon get up and stagger across the main road before running away between two warehouses. That little altar boy was certainly resourceful. Stuck in the middle of the street, the newly minted pedestrian lifted her arms to heaven, unable to process what had just happened to her. I was laughing like a kid, my foot pressing down on the accelerator. On the radio, Metallica was singing "Highway to Hell."

3

SUBTLETY

It's pretty hard for humans to be virtuous all the time; sometimes I even fall short myself. I was getting impatient at a red light, stuck behind a minivan, and rummaging through granny's glove compartment. Her purse had already blessed me with $344 and some shrapnel. I'd hit the jackpot! And here were a flashlight and a Swiss Army knife. They might come in handy at some point. I stashed my loot and felt a buzz as I kept an eye out for the fuzz. That was an awesome rhyme, so I wrote it down in my mental notebook for my rap album. As it happens, there was a sad lack of rap on the radio. I scanned through the frequencies and could only find insipid pop and nostalgic old rock. I'm a single-discipline artist. I only listen to—and produce—good rap. Even when I'm feeling very open-minded, all other music genres are basically shit. With just one exception, but I'm not going to tell you my favourite Francis Cabrel chansons.

In despair, I was starting in on my third loop through the radio stations when I heard my name. Dumbstruck, I turned my head to look at the back seat. Nobody there. They were talking about me on the radio! Already? They were even describing the red Echo I was using as a getaway car and the clothes I was wearing—my old grey Converse hoodie and pants. If only I'd known, I would have put on some proper threads.

I was famous! They were saying my name on the radio. And not just on any station, but on Radio-Canada, the federal mouthpiece. As the clip wound up with a typical national broadcaster ID, I was wavering between bursting with pride and imploding with panic. But this was no time to show off. I had to react quickly and think on my feet.

Horns were honking behind me, but I drove straight ahead at race pace, abandoning the car at the intersection. I had to get away from that car, as far and as fast as possible. I had absolutely no idea where I was. I couldn't remember having crossed the bridge so I must still be on the Île de Montréal. Maybe even right downtown, since the traffic was heavy and the sidewalks were crowded. I took the side streets, my feet pounding the asphalt, my lungs burning, but I didn't stop. I ran and ran until I got to the most surreal street in the world. Pink balls stretched across the horizon and covered the sky. There were garlands of these pastel-coloured balls everywhere I looked. I'd landed on planet gay: I was lost and panic-stricken, more vulnerable than a young female runaway on ecstasy at a rock concert.

It was no longer just a gay village in Montreal—the entire city of Montreal had become a queer paradise! Everywhere I looked, topless guys were holding hands with guys wearing cowboy hats. Ladies without an ounce of femininity were making out with other ladies. A window display filled with whips and torture implements utterly terrified me. I'd escaped from hell only to find myself sheltering in Sodom.

Even if it's not fashionable anymore, I remain fiercely heterosexual. I was soaked with sweat and completely out of breath.

I couldn't stay there, but I didn't have the strength to keep on running. Surrounded by a sea of queers, with no way out, I felt as though my physical and psychological integrity were under threat. They could be the kindest people in the world, and maybe I'm wrong to judge them, but I'd rather have a beam in my eye than a feather up my ass. I had to hide, and fast.

I was so happy to come across a store run by an Arab! Did you know that Arabs actually commit less crime on average than the population as a whole? His unexpected little souk represented my lifeline. I was so happy to get my hands on a cap, a change of clothes, and a knuckle-duster belt buckle that I could have kissed him.

He obligingly showed me how to get out of the area. I was desperate to cover up my tattoos as fast and as cheaply as possible. The dude advised me to head up toward Rue Ontario: *You can find everything there, my friend.*

I paid him what I owed and pulled my new Raptors cap down to my eyebrows. I took a deep breath and plunged back into Rue Sainte-Catherine's libidinous humidity. Poor Catherine, if she knew what was happening on the sidewalks named after her, she'd be hauling ass to decanonize herself.

I focused on the social housing on the horizon, walking as fast as I could without looking shifty. It was a bit slower than the ninja run, but faster than your average Joe Public. I overtook a few people and even passed a couple of police officers on bikes, too busy chatting about their collective bargaining agreement to pay any attention to me. Reassured, I pressed on, still thinking about my appearance: if I was going to wear urban camouflage, I might as well get pierced and tattooed at the same time. First I was thinking along the lines of a diamond teardrop with a fake diamond in it, but then a flash of genius hit me.

Everyone slows down at the sight of an accident but speeds up if someone asks them for help. The best way of getting ignored is to need other people.

At the corner of Ontario and Plessis, this revelation occurred to me when I spotted the most insignificant of all the anonymous punks. This young squeegee kid, rejected by all the drivers he was haranguing, his face marred by acne and grime, revealed my destiny to me. I had to become a punk. A Montreal punk, the most anonymous of all citizens from the dregs of society. Living on the margins of the marginalized, without identity or bills to pay.

Obviously I would need to dye my hair, cover up my amazing tattoos with anarchic scrawls, and hole up in the metropolis, even though I didn't speak English, the official language. I was going to adapt and disappear in the crowd while they looked for me in the surrounding areas, in my hometown, or in the villages where I was active. Good plan!

So I approached the dropout and offered him ten dollars to help me. Some people don't have much going on upstairs and some don't have anything going on. This guy was definitely one of the latter. Deep inside his pupils, whirling in the twists and turns of his irises, every cog turning in his head was visible in his eyes. If you looked a little further down, you could have seen them through his open mouth as well, but a thick tongue blocked the entrance. *Click!* The gear caught. He figured out I was serious when I offered him a purple-tinted portrait of John A. MacDonald. There wasn't much he wouldn't do for ten dollars. *Wow, ten bucks, man!* We were in business.

He started by introducing himself. His nickname made me

laugh, it was cool and original. It gave me a flash of inspiration for my own, right there and then. He thought mine was excellent and started using it deferentially. I had a new human resource on my hands. Despite looking like a dazed art teacher caught wanking to a high school yearbook, he might be useful. Vulnerable, potentially violent, and influenceable, I already liked Goofy.

Without going into details, I told him I wanted to live on the streets and needed the address of a cheap tattoo artist. When I saw the uneven tribal symbols peeking out from under his fraying T-shirt, I figured he knew someone very cheap.

You need Dumbo!

I respected his diagnosis and followed him.

It's not too far, Dumbo lives in a squat in an apartment in the east end, let's go!

Let's be clear: a psychiatric hospital is a micro-society with its own particular approach to cleanliness. Some cultures favour hygiene more than others. I was dirty, hairy, and unshaven: my metamorphosis into a punk wouldn't exactly be an extreme transformation.

We stopped at the drugstore on our way. We had to steal a good quality dye. My contractor convinced me it would be easy to make a crest on my head, a magnificent mohawk that fitted the code of the godless and lawless people on the margins of society. *You have a seriously good mop for that, bud. We'll get you an awesome ridge. Dumbo will have clippers.*

We stopped at the drugstore on our way. The other kind of drugstore this time: Stony McPebble's drugstore, reseller of rock, bud, ecstasy, and other self-ministered medications. Stony was the guy to know, harder to get around than an obese dead guy in a hallway: he had everything, or he could get his hands on it fast, with his commission on top.

The apartment was so dirty it was like being inside my own head. Half a dozen junkies shared the grey rug, puffing on glass pipes while a wrecked teenager snored on the sofa. An iguana was sleeping on his shoulder. I wanted to pinch the reptile or poke something in his eye just to see what would happen. Lizards don't react much to suffering, which I take as a personal challenge. But right then, there were too many witnesses stopping me from testing the animal's resilience. Too bad.

My minder invested six dollars in four orange pills that supposedly stimulated the central nervous system. *This is the real shit.* That was a pretty strong review of the product in question. I bought a dozen, along with some shatter, two grams of weed, and a last shot of cocaine. This stash would see me through to the end of the week. I was so happy to be able to get back to my old habits, to take up my old passion for psychoactive drugs. I was pretty emotional—I would have hugged Stony, but he wasn't very receptive. *Jesus, whoa, I barely know you!* I apologized and we continued our quest.

Wow, man, that is seriously fuckin' red. My new employee's voice dug its way out painfully from the prison of his clenched teeth. I was as buzzed as he was, my pupils so dilated that they were almost bigger than my irises, as I could see when I looked in the mirror. In the same reflection, behind me, my assistant repeated that I was kinda monochrome. For his part, Dumbo, an introverted young Mexican guy saddled with a funny nick-name, reassured me that this was the way to go. *Si, si, I know style, mano, I'm fucking Latino on both sides. No problemo with red, mano, it's the fashion!*

Dumbo was confirming my first impression: the best colour

for a redhead is red. My ten-inch mohawk looked pretty flashy, spiked with a fork and held in the air by beaten egg whites. And the crowning piece underneath this sublime crest, which wouldn't have been out of place on a show rooster, was my new tattoo: a scarlet target right in the middle of my forehead. Bang! Three concentric circles around a cross. I'd have given myself a merit certificate if I'd had one handy. Getting a tattoo on my head, like the MS-13 guys from Cuba, was a genius idea! It would intimidate people and direct their attention away from my face, if my new haircut didn't do the trick. And the people on the streets would take me seriously. Only the hardest of the hardcore get their faces tattooed.

To really confuse things, Dumbo modified the other works of art on my skin. My flaming Chinese character became a skull and crossbones, and the anagram of Edith, immortalized on my forearm, turned into a tribal symbol—a bit muddled but definitely transcendent, very contemporary art. The samurai on my back stayed untouched, I was hardly going to parade around town topless, right? With the two safety pins in my eyebrows and the one in my nostril, you'd have sworn I'd been a punk since the cradle.

After one last powder-enhanced joint we smoked together, I paid the artist, thanked my now-obsolete assistant, and started my street life. I didn't have a single dollar left in my pocket, but I had style, drugs, and freedom. That's more than any man needs to be happy.

The evening was going to be hotter than the embers of a blazing brothel. I was peaceful, still alone, but already a little less so. The field of possibilities had just grown by a few acres. I was out of jail, and so was my mother. I would find her first, then regain custody of my son. And, who knows, maybe even win back Edith's love.

I was so sure of the effectiveness of my disguise that I walked for hours. I had no idea where I was going but I was certainly determined to get there. I wanted to live, move, savour my release, totally exhilarated by my freedom. And a few grams of drugs.

I managed to collect a handful of change outside a liquor store. My urban camouflage worked amazingly well. Nobody dared look me in the eyes, so passersby either ignored me or stared at the puffy tattoo or the red crest towering over it. At five to eleven I went inside to buy a half litre of red. I had something to celebrate. Escaped, famous, tattooed, pierced, and dyed all in a single day; Houdini could get his coat—I was the king of escape now!

Being homeless in June is easier than being itinerant in December. Say what you like, but I reckon the vagabonds in Kuujjuaq are more deserving than the ones in Cancún. It's not a career choice that appeals much to me personally, but for the purposes of my escape, I needed the right street sense, like that guy Kenya West. It was already inspiring a chorus: *Cunning is dead in the street, fuck yeah, in the street you have to be crafty dead, braaaah, you will be dead, fuck yeah!* Fuck yeah, that's awesome urban poetry.

While I waited for the chance to turn my detailed observations into couplets, I was doing a bit of philosophizing. I thought about how you push your limits, you get pushed back, you get trampled on and misunderstood. You step even further back to make yourself believe it's not that bad, and then, the real cherry on the shitcake, you get trampled on even more. As I was reflecting, I wandered somewhere near Ontario and

Papineau. This was the epicentre of crooks, masseuses, sellers, buyers, renters, suckers, and a whole bunch of other screwed-up, or maybe totally fucked, people.

I was eager to spend my first night outside actually outside. Shutting myself up in a shelter or a squat was out of the question. I'd been dreaming of walking on the sidewalk for so long that I wasn't going to deny myself the pleasure. The streets were thronging with insignificant people, I wove in and out of them and did some reconnaissance: scouted out some depanneurs to rob, some spots for pissing. I was widening the perimeter, my calves were exhausted and my heels cracked, when I saw exactly what I needed to see.

When you're not going anywhere, the important thing is to know when to stop. As I was following a nice round ass under the stretched nylon of deliciously tight leggings, the oasis appeared to me. An enormous library rose up in front of me, the national library of Quebec. It was written there in big bronze letters that had been paid for by taxpayers who would never set foot inside it: Bibliothèque et Archives Nationales du Québec. I was so choked up by the sight that I immediately abandoned the delights of gazing at muscular butts to go and press my nose up against the glass door of this literary haven. It was closed, but it would open in a few hours. And it would be here all week long. I'd found my hideout nook: curled up with a library book. Books, carrels to be alone in, books, toilets for taking drugs, female students to ogle, books, computers to track down my mother, archives, comic books, books, books, and more books, everything I needed. It was a sign! Life seemed so beautiful I didn't even recognize it.

Happy as a fish in water, or a pedophile in a public swimming pool, I continued on my way. From the other side of the street, the bus terminal looked exotic. I went to the washrooms there and did a little line, a hint of cocaine, practically nothing at all, just enough to stay awake. At the exit there was a modest gathering of illegal immigrants, or people in the process of becoming such, sharing their poetry. Noting their formal use of words like *hot mess*, *muthafucka*, and *dope*, I figured they could be potential allies. I mingled among them.

I started a freestyle competition with the oldest of the Haitians, a big burly guy in his forties. I was on fire, I was totally getting the upper hand, even though nobody else thought so. One of his stooges called me a punk. Despite my appearance, that word was the final straw. I wanted to show him my irritation with a swift right hook to the jaw, but they all thought they were Mike Tyson. *Biff! Boff! Kapow!*

Hey, that's enough! Let him go!

I stood up quickly, barely even out of breath, since I'm used to tricky meetings. I was about to thank my good Samaritan when the colour of his uniform hit me even harder than the black guys had. A police officer. Worse still, one with a goatee. The lowest kind.

You okay? The big bastard was trying to soften me up.

Yeah, yeah, I need to go now, I'm in a hurry.

He smiled. *You have somewhere to be at two thirty in the morning? You meeting a dealer or an accountant?* He held me firmly by the arm; I tried in vain to detach myself.

I'm going to meet my sister, I'm staying with her tonight.

He lifted his right eyebrow skeptically, unconvinced. *Never seen you around here before. What's your name? Where you from?*

With the quickness of mind of a racing driver, I stated a false identity and said I'd just arrived from Rimouski. The constable put on his most pleased expression. *The Bas-du-Fleuve shrimp are in season!*

I shrugged my shoulders. *I wouldn't know, I prefer steak.*

He let me go. *Alright, off you go to find the other summer punks. Try to avoid getting beaten up in the future. We won't always be there.*

Pretty relieved that my disguise had worked, I set off without hurrying, proud of having scammed a police officer but hurt at having been attacked by some hip-hop brothers. Clothes maketh not the man, for fuck's sake! They should have been able to tell I was a professional rapper even though I was wearing this punk getup. No way was it a bad enough crime for them to set the whole gang on me, even Cain would never have been that disloyal (the murderer, not the band). But I wasn't going to let these kids' lack of solidarity discourage me. On the contrary. The good thing about getting stabbed in the back is that it gives you some forward momentum.

I spared a thought for Simon. He must have felt kinda betrayed when I pushed him into the road. We rarely get what we deserve, even when we deserve the worst. On the worst nights, I console myself by remembering that every single one of us is a dirty-fucking-dog-who-deserves-a-slow-and-painful-death for *someone*. Nobody's perfect.

I needed to sit down, find somewhere quiet, out under the stars, to get through the night and avoid the fuzz. Habitually speaking, humans are creatures of habit, it's well-documented. I turned onto Rue Ontario in the hope of finding my punk buddy or a hideout for the night. I was keeping a sharp eye out. They say that a good night's sleep brings clarity, but in that neighbourhood a good night's sleep was more likely to bring a knife between my ribs.

The fauna had changed, and they were smoking some quality flora. There were a lot of different herds in my field of vision, each with its own aroma, or not. By the door of a bar, old white people my age were making out with their own youthful selves, smoking, laughing as if life was great. A more realistic trio of drunks were puffing on cancer sticks nearby. Their scrawny dog started yowling when some other punk's dogs started yapping. The alkies yelled at the punk, who wasn't impressed. Farther away, some prostitutes were having a heated discussion about their commercialization strategies. A woman's gotta do what a woman's gotta do to survive, after all.

This isn't your beat, you old scrap-heap whore, this is the trans area! The small Asian woman's deep, gravelly voice surprised me.

The other woman, way drunker, replied with slurred dignity, *This is my spot, so shut your mouth, you fucking psychopath bastard!*

The newcomer took her elder's advice and trotted a few metres along the street. Now that she was absolute master of her patch of sidewalk, the bargain-basement prostitute was simpering at every car that deigned to slow down. Life had driven over her body, overloaded and with nailed tires, and then reversed over it again for good measure. She was a real street whore, with all the cracks and the lived-in look of the dilapidated buildings of the metropolis. Like the Olympic Stadium, she was in desperate need of being patched up, repaired, loved a little. But it was too late. She would never love herself again. She had to stay intoxicated, it was too painful to let herself come down. With a heart full of chilblains and her head perforated from the inside, dope was the only thing keeping her upright—and on her knees. Drugs can be powerful stuff. Especially on Rue Ontario.

I leaned against the wall of a diner, crouching in the shadow of the doorway, and watched her routine. Like someone on an urban safari, I analyzed the wild animal's behaviour. The winks at the passersby, the nervous glances at the cops, the furtive swigs from the bottle. Stereotypical, commonplace, and extraordinary. Although I couldn't figure out why, I recognized myself in her.

I have to admit, the old lady fascinated me. She was upright and destroyed at the same time. She radiated the beauty of a decrepit barn, the kind people take artsy black-and-white photos of. But in colour, she was resplendent and ravaged. Whores get worn out more quickly than women who do it for free. They sell their asses but they can't buy back their youth. Creams do nothing. The time spent cruising the sidewalk ends up inside their bodies, just like a stranger's penis. Occupational hazard.

The summer night's electric atmosphere was fading, and the people passing by, even the hot babes in leggings, left me indifferent. My gaze lingered on the woman behind the prostitute. Because there was indeed a woman. The more I scrutinized her face, the more I had the feeling I knew her, I recognized her. Deep down, she was like me. A fighter, knocked down a thousand times but undaunted, still there, still standing in the upheaval, noble and misunderstood. And a bit of a redhead too.

I wanted her so much, but just in a gentle way. I yearned to rest my head on what was left of her chest, hold her in my arms, let her rub my back, kiss her fraternally, and tell her that everything would be fine: *Yes, everything will be fine.* I decided to slip out of the shadows and approach her, offer her a joint, a sip of wine, a hug, anything she wanted, but a souped-up Toyota Celica with tinted windows beat me to it. Without even negotiating through the window like they do in documentaries, she got into the car and they drove off eastward, leaving me behind. My heart turned upside down; I stretched out my hand after her in vain.

There is nothing pure in this world. Even virgin forests are crawling with bugs. If you're friendless and loveless, what's the meaning of life? Even asking the question is a way of avoiding answering it. I was seriously down and pretty much ready to sink into a major depression. I would have liked to eject myself from my head, but it wasn't time for escaping anymore, I had to square up to my destiny—and smash its face in.

Where should I start? My revenge list was so crowded that I couldn't even hope to get through it without attracting police attention. Edith and my son must be living in a witness protection program. And there was no one to console or advise me, even the mysterious, magnetic sex worker had slipped through my fingers.

Suddenly, I don't know why, while my mind was lingering on the vanished old lady, I thought of my mother. Mama was close by; I could feel it in my gut. I had to figure out where she lived, find her city, her street, and the meaning of my life. Fuck my son, fuck my ex, fuck my vendettas, and fuck the black hole trying to suck me in. I would worry about the existential details later. Right now I needed to find love, the only love capable of reconciling me with my life, satisfying me on all fronts—intellectual, sexual, and emotional: I was going to track down my mother. Once and for all.

4

CHARITY

Contrary to how it might look today, Émilie Gamelin wasn't a crackhead who sold her ass to buy rocks. She was a saintly woman, the founder of a religious clique that was very prosperous back in the day. Rich enough for its matriarch to bequeath her name to the coolest square in the city. Émilie Gamelin Park is the place to be when you have nowhere else to be.

Since dawn it's been swarming with everything the night spat up on the city sidewalks. Unfulfilled sex maniacs, starving people so disillusioned they would tear angels limb from limb to get a bucket of spicy wings. Everyone had something to sell, often themselves, so they could buy what the others were selling. Whether it was to get one last hit before they crashed or a first shot to start the day off, the sunrise gathered together junkies of every stripe.

An addict is a trapped animal. But instead of gnawing off its paw to free itself, it licks the snare imprisoning it. My head was spinning as I tried to follow the whole merry-go-round of scams and other transactions. Drug addiction is a demanding hobby.

I stayed there for hours, smoking cigarettes, refusing sandwiches from social workers, wondering if the police were actively looking for me. Even if they were trying to hunt me down, they wouldn't recognize me. The jovial police officers on their bikes zigzagged through the park without paying me much attention. They were focusing on the more violent guys. I had no energy. Like the Arctic, I was visibly melting. I was less muddled from the medication, which was a good thing, but I was also losing the comforting stupor of drunkenness, which was bad.

Two social workers and a churchy do-gooder came around one by one to offer me a listening ear. It was pretty obscene the way they prowled from one desperate person to the next. They could lay on the goodwill as thick as they liked, I didn't buy it. Nobody is disinterested, and I refused to let them make a profit off my back. Maybe I'm prejudiced. Not all priests are child molesters, and not all Italians are in the Mafia, sure. But you have to admit that Italian priests are pretty suspect. Especially when they get involved in peewee hockey, scouts, or any other professional pedophile organization. Unfrocked or not, these hip pastors don't fill me with confidence. A social worker is a predator just like everyone else, just better disguised and sneakier. Nobody does anything for anybody for nothing.

I didn't need any professionals to get myself going, nor any intervention plans, care workers, or priests. In life, you can choose whether you see the glass as half-empty or half-full, or whether you get up and fill it up or smash it and open your veins with it. You always have a choice.

At last, the time came. My national library was about to open. I fixed my hair and dragged my unslept carcass to the Holy Grail. Rereading old Bukowski would sort my ideas out, and if not, at least his famous nymphettes would distract me.

On the front page! My giant face covered two-thirds of the *Journal de Montréal*. I was so stunned I could have fainted on the library table. Instead, I sat down. *Dangerous Murderer Escapes from Pinel*, in huge red letters. Same colour, the subtitle just below read: *Are We Safe?* Now, that's what you call obtaining your letters of nobility.

I could already see myself on the big screen. I'd be a famous celebrity! Imbued with wisdom, I tried to stay humble, but it was all just so gratifying. Except for the fact that the photo was kinda dated now. I was young, skinny, long-haired, freshly injected, and beaten up by the Pinel agents. I looked crazy. It was annoying, but I consoled myself with the thought that it looked so unlike me that nobody would be able to identify me from that photo. Nor from the photos of my tattoos; they'd already been modified. Bravissimo me!

The article was full of praise, they said I was very dangerous and unpredictable. They mentioned my feats of arms, my escapades and my youthful indiscretions, and my operating methods, which they called modus operandi for their Latino readers. They laid out the details of my escape. Sadly, Marcel was on the mend, Jamal too. But their union had condemned their working conditions and would continue to increase the pressure, blah blah blah. Those communists never miss a trick.

Right at the end of the article, I was overjoyed to learn that Simon had been captured. My formidable accomplice. After less than ten hours of freedom, he'd been picked up in the early evening, in tears, kneeling in blood on the steps of the Oratoire Saint-Joseph. Holy bloody Simon!

The library had been heaving with people since it opened, which was nice to see. Especially the schoolgirls in their uniforms, cute little budding members of the bourgeoisie. With socks up to their knees and skirts up to their asses, they smelled richly of youthful eroticism. There were more experienced cégep girls too; in fact, there were so many women of all kinds, I didn't know where to look first. An athletic woman wearing leggings and reaching up as she stood on tiptoe. A secretary wearing fishnet stockings, browsing through the bottom shelf. There was even a chubby employee sticking her tongue out as she lapped at the water fountain. There was a lot of emotion going on under the fly for an escaped inmate. It was hard on the retina. I had to relieve my innermost thoughts in the public washrooms, sometimes four or five times a day. Damn, women are beautiful!

The library was also full of foliage among the roses—art students, dozens of them, leafing through massive coffee-table books that were *For Reference Only*. People make a big deal about Jean-Paul Riopelle, but let's be clear: in terms of both stencils and graffiti, we've seen better. I really liked looking up the old French painters, especially Picasso and the other immigrants in his clique. They had real talent in that group, they didn't just share a love of absinthe. Especially Degas—the guy was permanently hammered, suffering from syphilis, and hanging out with dancers, but it didn't stop him from getting his art recognized.

Speaking of old things, there were a ton of retirees browsing the shelves too. Geriatrics trying to lose their loneliness in the pages of the great classics. And to round out the picture, a whole bunch of people from many different ethnic groups. Everyone loves a free service!

I'd typed and retyped Mama's name and initials, but not a single website would reveal her address to me. That would have been too easy. Even if I had found her, it might just have turned out to be some other smartass like that crazy lady in Sherbrooke. My noble quest was just starting. I'd find a way to flush Mama out in due course.

While I waited, I went from one floor to the next looking for newspapers, curious to see if I was in them. Nothing in *Le Devoir*, obviously: they don't really cover anything except the rantings of left-wing separatists. I carried on looking. *La Presse* had relegated me to page sixteen, but still, that was pretty good for a newspaper aimed at anglophile intellectuals. The *La Presse* reporter made much of one crucial aspect of my massive file: no recent photos, no personal information, and no sample in the DNA database.

The report gave an overview of the holes in the system that meant that individuals who had been judged not criminally responsible did not have to be included in the criminal database. The appendix to Article 16 was very clear on this point: an individual who is not criminally responsible for his actions cannot be recorded as a criminal. And I was just one of many such cases.

Without this information, capturing me would be more difficult and, especially in the event of violent recidivism, there would be no opportunity for genetic matching. My situation in particular was interesting because I had, in fact, been criminally convicted: my DNA should have been collected while I was incarcerated in prison. But because of the slowness of bureaucracy, or more likely typical civil-servant laziness, this vital swab had not been taken. Because of this, my recapture might be in jeopardy. *And if the Pinel escapee commits another crime, this is going to blow up into a large-scale political scandal.*

Ha! I'll be committing it, my dears; prepare the scandal, I'll be committing another crime! Carried away by excitement, I was whispering out loud. Two old fogeys and an art history student glared at me. All it took was a grunt from me to send them back to their books. If an honest man can't be enthusiastic in peace, what's the world coming to?

I had to sort my mind out and get my breath back. How could I optimize my new popularity and exploit my platform without getting arrested? Such dizzyingly fast celebrity can cause problems for a man who needs to operate anonymously. I had all the charm of Ted Bundy, which would be useful, but I didn't want to get stupidly caught like he did. Escaping is one thing, but staying escaped is another matter entirely.

I cut out the articles feverishly. I hadn't expected to have such a big media impact so soon, it was exhilarating. Reaching the top is admirable. Reaching it by way of a detour through skid row is even more impressive. I have to admit, I was even kind of a fan of myself. But for now I had to keep a low profile, master my territory, and enjoy my freedom.

A security guard yanked me out of my slumber and out of the pool of drool my head was resting in. My body was rigid, I'd been having a premonitory nightmare of never waking up again. How many hours had I been sleeping there, slumped on this table? It was hard to say, but enough to sober me up completely and stiffen me up. I almost fell over as I tried to stand. My balance was out of whack, victim of my painful muscles and medication withdrawal. What they give you at Pinel isn't just pretty candy. I was as pale as the Joker. I needed to knock back some speed, smoke a few grams, and have a good strong drink, stat.

The guard escorted me to the door. He was enjoying kicking me out way too much. My surveillance of the library had shown me that there were around a dozen guards permanently stationed over the four floors of the building and the two floors of underground parking. Not much to cover a building of that size, especially when you consider their size and their weapons: they were just a bunch of small-town rednecks and failed athletes with walkie-talkies working for Garda. And they were tolerant too, they only kicked out the homeless and other marginalized people when there were unbearable smells, fights, or snoring, as in my case. In light of these facts, I congratulated myself for having spotted the building during my first few hours of escape, and I let myself be escorted out with the firm resolve of coming back sooner rather than later.

The best thing about buying a bottle of alcohol is the opportunity it gives you to steal a second bottle. With two litres of Baby Duck in hand, I could look forward to the rest of the day with a sense of peace. I abandoned my begging spot outside the liquor store and headed to the park to enjoy the sun as it set between the buildings. I was savouring the twilight when a brunette with green roots approached me.

What's your name?

Wow, she was coming on strong. *None of your business. What's yours?*

She stuck her face in mine, the way Americans plant their flag on conquered territory. *Bébette, and I'm thirsty.*

I like a woman who knows what she wants, especially when she wants the same thing as me.

Punks like to conform even more than soldiers, and Bébette had the full uniform: eighteen-hole Docs, ripped tights, Ramones T-shirt under a jacket covered in badly sewn-on badges, and a clump of hair in the approved colour. But she also had a pretty face, and some contours under her sweater. Her breasts were making me promises my patience wouldn't be able to keep. I let her sit down next to me.

I held out the brown bag to her, and she took a big slug from the bottle.

Hold your horses, Jack Kerouac, you're supposed to enjoy it slowly.

She wiped her lips on her jacket. *Jack who?*

I took a swig myself. *Never mind, I read too much… Have you ever noticed we don't use the word swig enough?*

She smiled. *Jesus, you really do read too much. Give me some more of that!*

Letting a woman drink is an investment in the future. I uncorked the second bottle while she was parroting her soporific revolutionary speech, getting worked up about multinationals, oil companies, threatening to blow the whole lot sky-high. She quoted Norman Chomsky at me and spouted endless bits from Naomi Klein's books. She really believed in her utopian pablum with a side of class struggle. A punk who dreams of revolution is about as harmless as a leftist with a humanities degree. I let her rant and even offered to go to the next protest with her. We were putting the world to wrongs between sips of wine.

Showing a commendable sense of initiative, Bébette suggested we go and screw. She even used the word screw, which struck me as very promising. Since she deserved some positive reinforcement, I offered her the last glug of the vino. *I'm ready, where shall we go?* Totally ignoring her own environmental beliefs, she threw the bottle under a bush and told me to follow her. She had a luxury place for doing it. And that too.

Since we had to go by Rue Ontario anyway, I asked Bébette if we could make a detour by the corner of Papineau. Why did I want to see the old prostitute again? I have no idea, or at least only bad ideas. Especially since I had a definitely fuckable punkette offering me her firm twenty-year-old body, and I should have been burning rubber to go and fuck her. But you can't control magnetism, and I wanted to see if my lady of the night felt it, if our eyes would meet and our gazes would communicate. Bébette told me the woman's name was Maple. Miss Maple, the neighbourhood veteran. The woman was both irritating and irritable, and totally out of her mind. *She's more explosive than downtown Lac Mégantic*, Bébette warned me.

Bébette didn't understand what I could possibly see in her either, but there are forces of attraction—karmic links or sexual deviancy—that are stronger than us. There's nothing we can do about it. It's just the way it goes.

One cigarette later, Bébette was getting impatient. *This has to happen like now or it's not going to happen at all.*

She really had my little devil by the horns here, so I fell into step behind her and followed her body; I'd already put nearly a litre of good wine into it and I wasn't about to lose my investment. We headed north again, onto Lorimier. We warmed each other up with licks and curious fingers, pausing now and again to promise each other dirty things. She stared at me, grabbed my balls, nibbled my thumb. From her lusty expression, I could see this wasn't her first rodeo. *Get over here! I want some dick!* The dick in question was practically jumping out of its skin to volunteer.

I followed her to the beautifully worked door of a stone building. *Christ, girl, you've got some money!*

Bébette knelt down, and I thought she was going to suck me off right there on the front steps. But I was disappointed; she pulled two bobby pins out of her pocket and set about picking the lock. This hot pussy was also an accomplished cat burglar. This was fantastic; she was climbing to new heights in my estimation. *You have every single good quality in the world!*

Her aphrodisiac face lit up and she pushed open the door with a little wiggle of her ass.

Some people make love, others fuck, some screw, and others masturbate inside their partner. It's all a question of your relationship or otherwise with the other person. I never really knew where I fit in, I was lost, adrift, distressed.

Suddenly my eyes were wetter than Vandal Vyxen, and I was crying like the Trevi Fountain. It was running into Bébette's face and onto the floor. Was I going crazy right now, developing a serious mental problem? I couldn't screw any longer, I was cut off mid-flow, lying across Bébette, who was herself stretched out on the hardwood floor in this big, empty apartment. Empty like me.

Not all naked women are pleasant discoveries—sometimes you even want to send them away to cover themselves up—but Bébette was sublime. She was the most beautiful sex volunteer I'd ever seen. In a well-proportioned apartment that was as bare as she was, it was just all too much beauty. When it came to women, I always hoped for the moon but expected to have to settle for a flickering fluorescent bulb. When she dropped her jacket and skirt, then pulled off her T-shirt to reveal her body in the lamplight, I was flabbergasted. This was getting close to the mystical. It hit me right in the gut, tied my heart in a knot, this girl was like a sculpture!

In the middle of a pared-down room, haloed by the street lights, she was had something of the surrealism of a statue, and I no longer dared touch her. Not a single tattoo, scar, or stretch mark betrayed her humanness. Not even a lopsided nipple to spoil the portrait. Bébette's breasts were as firm as her political convictions. She was as splendid as a Photoshopped supermodel who'd invested thousands in surgical enhancement—but she was real. I had to focus on what we'd promised each other; I had to fucking desanctify her as fast as I fucking could.

Bébette lay down gracefully on her back on the varnished wood. She spread her perfect thighs, placed her perfect fingers on her hairy muff. Maybe the fur was a nod to Frida Kahlo. But even the fuzzy bush was perfect. It was incredibly concealing and added a hint of wildness to this untamed beauty. I flung off my dirty shorts, my even dirtier underwear, and stretched out on top of this woman the way a poem stretches out on the page.

A few lines of verse came to my lips, so I recited them for her. Women love erotic poetry just as they're about to do the deed, it's well-documented in a special edition of *Chatelaine*. *Your adorable hole lifts me to the skies, to clouds of exaltation.* Apparently she wasn't a Leonard Cohen fan. She just stuck her tongue in my mouth and pressed her body against mine.

She must have known the power of her taut skin and her disturbing shabby-sexy chic. Without any further foreplay, she wrapped her hand around my rod and jammed it inside her: *Get on with it, stick it in, Mr. Intellectual.* I didn't want to laugh anymore, I didn't want anything anymore. I was floating inside my overly spacious head, I was wandering lost in the desert of her clavicle. Her pussy was hot and soft, like wet velvet but better. Finally I had a place to call my own. I could climb in and take shelter, her vagina was taking me in its arms.

We danced a little, but Bébette wanted to screw, and she couldn't care less about the rest of the flesh around the boner. *Come on, fuck me!* I was both inside her and thousands of kilometres away at the same time, nowhere. My face crumpled up and I wept. She was focused on her pelvis, but I was out of my depth. I was sobbing. I was suffocating.

I can stroke your back if you want, but take your dick out first or it's gonna be way too weird. I stubbornly wanted to concentrate on the task at hand, to grit my teeth and fuck like a man, but I was bawling like a little girl. And those are two things it's pretty tricky to do at the same time.

After an hour, Bébette was fed up. She was thirsty too, what with the constant gushing from my taps that wouldn't turn themselves off. Apparently the body is seventy per cent tears, so I had to be on the point of drying up. But still, without knowing why, nor where it was all coming from, it continued to flow with no sign of running dry. *You can squat here for the night if you want, it's warm and I need fresh air, but you have to leave before eight in the morning, they come and visit sometimes.* Bébette had a real sense of hospitality.

I watched her getting dressed again. It was already over. The world is so ugly that I wanted to rinse my eyes with her beauty. Naked, unarmed, and in the throes of emotion, I wasn't exactly overconfident. I have no idea how much time passed over my body. But when I stood up I was cold, and the crazy pins and needles in my legs accompanied my loneliness. Loneliness is kinda stupid as an emotion, since we're all always alone anyway. I was too alone for my taste, standing in front of the finely crafted mirror in the bathroom. I stared at myself with my red eyes. You can't deny the evidence or deny your own face: I was old. Old and emotional. The truth was right there on my forehead: my tattoo was scarring over faster than I was. Even guys who have tempered steel rocks for hearts have emotions. No need to get dramatic about it or start doubting myself. *When you're moving forward, the important thing is never to take a step back*, as Virginia Plath might have said if those rocks hadn't dragged her down.

I had a shower and didn't sing at all, then dried myself off with the curtain in the master bedroom. I had to pull myself together as quickly as possible, get out of there, find some alcohol or find Bébette again, and get her to give me a second chance. After all, we'd been through something big together.

5

MODERATION

On the Road is a load of shit. I mean, Kerouac didn't even have a car. Anyway, as he would say in his crappy French, the reality of escape is less romantic than it is in novels. It becomes a burden, having to find food, drugs, places to crash for the night, and other places to take a shit. I'd only been on the streets for two days but I'd already done the tour. Freedom is destabilizing: you have to remember to eat and sleep, you can smoke whenever you want. I was smoking too much. I wanted to move on to something else, get settled: vagrancy doesn't lead anywhere. I was hoping to find Bébette again, propose that we move in together and start a family or some other similar project.

Maple got dropped off at the corner of Champlain. I noticed her from a distance, I'd been wandering up and down Ontario since dawn, smoking cigarette butts and getting in some rap practice. With a bit of distance, I can admit I'd been hoping to see her again. I couldn't escape the feeling that she was the one my destiny was tied to.

She was coming back from doing her night shift just as day was breaking, in big grey strips of cloud, and cold mist that clung to our bodies. Staggering toward me, Maple was trying to light her smoke, but the high heels of her pink leopard-print boots made balancing difficult. She was colourful from head to toe, especially the head. She had a peroxide mop going from yellow to six inches of grey-and-red regrowth. She must have been forty-nine, but she looked sixty-three. You age fast in the prostitution industry, it's a physical job, demanding and well-documented.

A sad sun was rising in her drooping face. She pulled out a pair of big round smoked glasses from her tired mauve purse. What class, she walked right by me without even looking at me, a real street diva. I grasped hold of my courage with both hands and politely called out to her. *Yo, Maple!*

She swung around slowly, like a bus turning on a dime, pushed her glasses down with a badly manicured index finger, then stared at me with her rust-brown eyes. *Whaddya want?*

Good point, what did I want? *Do you have a cigarette, please?*

She came closer, sucked a long drag on her king-size, then blew the smoke in my face. *Sorry, I don't smoke.*

I was overwhelmed by her face, which was twenty-two inches away from mine; she was having even more of an effect on me than Bébette did, but in a different way. I was all inside-out like a dirty sock. This whore was a mystery to be solved, I needed to figure out why she made my soul vibrate so much. *I-I j-just wanna tell you…*

What, kiddo, what do you wanna tell me?

You could have cut the silence with a chainsaw. My whore was about to take off, I had to act. *I-I want to talk to you.*

Her breath hit me in the face. *Hahaha!* I liked her raucous laugh already. She put a hand on my shoulder and moved closer. *Talking takes more effort than anything else, kiddo. You're gonna have to pay for it!*

Mama must have seen the newspapers. She must be worried, with everything they'd written about me, a shit ton of half-truths scattered among the outright lies. And police violence must worry her too—I could have been injured when I was arrested. But nothing can stop me now. I've regained my freedom and sooner or later I will find my progenitrix.

While I waited to begin the steps of hunting her down, I tried to find money for Maple. Thirty bucks would guarantee me a good half-hour of chat or head (no teeth). I didn't doubt her fellatory expertise, but I was saving my pennies to have a chat with her. I had this feeling that she had a lot to teach me, like an oracle or a fortune teller. This woman possessed a truth that was still escaping me. She must have read all the books about personal growth, she gave off such an air of confidence.

When you are begging, the main thing is to be pitiful, to inspire pity, not so much to make people feel charitable as to avoid making them feel the opposite. Nothing sickens a good bourgeois soul in a hurry like a cheerful beggar. You always need someone to be needier than you are. We have to offer up our distress to them, show that we're way more unhappy than they are, if we want to make them want to shower all their money down on our misery.

Just like with the fingers on our hands, it's often the coarsest people who stand head and shoulders above the rest. And politeness is a sign of weakness. I never say thank you or please to anyone. Inspiring pity is one thing, but I don't want people trampling on my pride. *Gimme a buck... I know you have some, give me some cash...* Even when you're standing by a meter maid it takes a long time to collect thirty dollars in shrapnel. Especially as lunchtime was approaching and I needed to eat too. I was regretting spending all my loot and taking all my drugs in two days. Like a gambler or a limp dick, I needed to get a little reinforcement. Determined to demonstrate my entrepreneurial nature, I went straight to the source, into the middle of the street, to bang on drivers' windows and brandish my cardboard cup under their noses. *Come on, I have cancer, give me something to eat!*

A big sucker in an oversized current-model chrome-plated truck is still a big sucker. The fancy carriage doesn't change anything, but somehow it doesn't stop illiterate social climbers from thinking they're Cinderella. You should haver seen that guy pushing me down off his footboard, treating me like a pauper.

Wealth is on the inside, jerk, you have to look at life through your heart's eyes!

Unconvinced, he gave me nothing. Nor did the lady in the Tercel behind him, nor the teen in the Corolla, nor the retired guy in the CRV, and I just got one measly dollar from the sweetheart in the Jetta. It made me want to play American roulette, which is pretty much the same as the Russian version, but the cylinder is full and you fire straight into the crowd.

I tried again a block over. Forty-five cents! This was too much. If society was refusing to help me, I'd just have to steal from society. End of story. I'd given society a chance, now it needed to pull its socks up.

I wouldn't go so far as to say I was the incarnation of virtue or Robin Hood reincarnated, but I do have values. When it's time to commit a crime, I take stock of the moral parameters. After all, I could have held up a fair-trade business, a food bank, or a co-op, but I chose a 7-Eleven.

If you're going to attack capitalism, you might as well assault a multinational worthy of the name. Bébette would approve. Not only had 7-Eleven forced all the mom-and-pop stores—except the few Asian-owned ones that still remained—to close down, but, even worse, they sell junk food, from slushies to jujubes to hot dogs. Hot dogs at the convenience store? Surely that's one of the signs of societal collapse! Even homeless people won't eat them, so you have to wonder where they find those bulimics willing to stuff their faces with the scraps from the slaughterhouse floor. Anyway, I was taking on the duty of condemning their hegemonic monopoly by going to lighten the till at their store at the bottom of Rue Saint-Denis. I was all set to leave with my hands full and to murder rampant neo-liberalism. As Tommy Douglas, a notorious communist, used to say, *You don't win a battle with slogans and placards, for Christ's sake, you just need the right person to bleed at the right time!*

First up, I had to get hold of a working uniform for the job. Since I still wanted to hide out in the neighbourhood, it would be better to work anonymously. Even more so now that my amazing urban camouflage could work against me: having a target on your forehead makes you pretty identifiable.

Criminality is just a branch of business like any other. You have to take risks, develop your expertise, and know how to intelligently reinvest in your assets. I gathered up my eight dollars and ten cents in change and dived into the first thrift store I passed. They didn't have any balaclavas. I know the Zapatista movement isn't that active in Montreal, but surely it ought to be pretty easy to get hold of a balaclava in any self-respecting store! The lady threatened to call the police if I didn't calm down. I calmed down. She was a saleswoman through and through, so she helped me find a tuque big enough to be used as a balaclava. It was fluorescent orange and came down to the middle of my chin—not exactly ideal. I took it anyway, with a pair of cord pants and a T-shirt with some joke about golfers on the front. I still had two dollars left. *Cha-ching!*

The little penknife I'd found in the Echo's glove compartment would do the trick. Knives are like penises: it's not size that matters, it's what you do what it. Adrenaline is a good substitute for stimulant drugs: sweaty hands, highly strung nerves. I was pretty out of it, soaring as high as Baudelaire's albatross. In the library washrooms I managed to crush my mohawk, which was already losing its freshness, to stuff it more effectively into my balaclava. Reclothed, hairstyled, and determined, I set off toward wealth.

It was lunch break on Saint-Denis. In the June sunshine, patios were crammed full of small-time bosses with their mistresses dangling on their arms. The sidewalks were overflowing, which was perfect, it would help me ensure a sneaky escape by blending in with the crowd. I furtively prepared my weapon. *Shit, that's the bottle opener, that's the nail file, that's the screwdriver. Fucking Swiss people!* I eventually managed to get the blade out. With my makeshift balaclava covering my face down to my chin, I pushed open the door to the store, brandishing my weapon.

Motherfucker, it was crammed full of people. There was a long line at the cash and customers all over the place. I quickly pulled my balaclava back up and hightailed it out of there. Shame. But as all the dragons, drug dealers, and other businessmen will tell you, if you can't manage to break into one market, you have to attack another one.

Mrs. Wong was serving her only customer, a puny child of twelve, when I went in. So no danger on that front, but I took note of him anyway. Maybe he was related to the owner. But I didn't have time to waste tracing his family tree back, so I yelled at the kid to lie down on the ground and brandished my blade under Mama Miyagi's nose. *Gimme the cash!*

That cow did not respect all the details of the Quebec Business Council's recommendations. Instead of giving me money, she landed me a punch in the throat. The throat! Fucking kung fu. It was the kind of punch that knocks the breath out of you. I tripped over the kid stretched out on the floor and banged the back of my head on the liquor fridge. Struggling to breathe, stretched out full-length on the floor, I suddenly found myself more vulnerable than Christopher Reeve in a horse race.

The woman grabbed the telephone fixed to the wall. Now this was going too far. Hitting me was one thing, but calling the police on me was another. I could have fled right then, but she was seriously overexaggerating—I hadn't even stolen anything from her yet.

In one leap, I launched myself at her, trampling the child on the ground underfoot, collateral damage. She let go of the handset to protect her face with two hands. My blade sliced into her left palm like a knife through butter. Or more like butter that you forgot to take out of the fridge before the meal. Anyway, my little penknife stayed stuck in place. The woman screamed in pain. She launched herself backwards, taking my weapon with her. We both stared at her bleeding hand, with the Swiss Army knife embedded in it. *Hey, give me my knife back!*

With the grace of an antelope, she got herself out from behind the counter and started running through the store. She'd obviously read Lao Tzu's *The Art of War*, and I had to admire her withdrawal strategy. I immediately chased after her, she forked off down one aisle and then another. The kid seized his chance during this exciting pursuit to save himself too, shrieking *Pidaaah, Piiiidaaah!* as he ran. He was going to bring the whole neighbourhood out to riot. Everything that could go wrong was about to go even wronger. Out of breath, I stopped to propose a deal. *Madam, if you give me my knife back, I'll go, I promise.*

She was furious. *Go! Get the fuck out of here!*

Hmm, she was clearly better integrated than I'd first thought. She probably supported Quebec independence too. Pierre Falardeau would have been proud. That movie he made about not caring whether people were white, black, yellow, or green with orange polka dots as long as they wanted Quebec to become its own continent was really popular for a while.

Yes, ma'am, I'll get the fuck out of here, but I want my knife first!

She was clutching her injured hand, with blood flowing faster and faster, spraying over the lino back and forth like a metronome.

I need it. Give it back and then I'll go, spit-swear. As a gesture of good faith, I spat on her counter.

She started yelling even more in a Chinese dialect. I was about to give chase again, determined to recover my possession, when an enormous dude appeared at the back of the store. Actually, he was smaller than me, but I suspected he was a martial arts pro like his mama.

Abandoning my balaclava as I ran, I climbed the fences of two buildings, plunged into the crowd, and went to catch my breath in an underground parking lot, safely away from the yellow peril. What a disastrous operation: I'd come away without the loot, and without even my balaclava and my knife. I tried to philosophize to boost my morale. That's life, it's often a lose-lose situation.

Reading might be food for the soul, but the body cannot sustain itself on photos of Martha Stewart's fancy salads alone. In the middle of the afternoon, I planned to leave the national library. Hunger and thirst were gnawing away at my insides, and I knew my punk clothes would guarantee my anonymity. From the enormous windows on the second floor, I could see the police officers gradually getting scarcer in the surrounding streets. They were slowly abandoning the search.

My own research, conducted on an incredibly slothful and overused computer, did nothing to reassure me. Somehow they already suspected me of the attack on the Chinese convenience store. How had they guessed? *Breaking news: the killer who escaped from Pinel is still in Montreal.* My photo was everywhere, and people were asked to contact the police if they saw me, since I was known to be very dangerous and armed. Those fascists were exaggerating. Mrs. Wong was never in any danger. And on top of that, she'd kept my knife, so now I wasn't even armed anymore!

I cast one last look down at the crowded street. I could only spot one short arm of the law, so I decided I could finally go out and eat. On the already crowded table, I placed my current reading material: *One Flew Over the Cuckoo's Nest*, a poignant true story.

In the glass elevator, a single mother and her two pre-schoolers stared at me, or rather at my forehead. I grimaced to make them laugh. It didn't exactly work: the smaller girl started sobbing like a little kid. This was a bad day all round. With the stiff upper lip of an Irishman, I kept my smile pasted on and acknowledged the security guard posted at the entrance. *See you soon, Nestor!*

In the trash can outside Chez Amir, I unearthed half a falafel sandwich and a bunch of hash browns. As Gordon Ramsay says, *As long as it fills your stomach, who cares if it tastes like crap?* I took as much as I could carry, and there was still some left, but an employee came to chase me away. It was humiliating. It's bad for your self-esteem to be caught rummaging through trash cans, but it's good for the environment. And less hassle than planting a tree. So, despite my shame I congratulated myself.

In the park, I wandered around as I ate at the speed of an eighty-year-old on morphine. The punch in the throat had seriously hampered my ability to swallow. I hoped I might find Bébette around the metro station, when the evidence jumped at my face like a pit bull attacking a child: I needed a dog. The vast majority of punks lying around the park had one or even two. I didn't know whether the SPCA would give me a former-employee discount, but I didn't have time to schlep over to the other side of town to find out. I had to get my outfit completed ASAP. It was about credibility. If I wanted to be a textbook punk, I needed to be poor, badly tattooed, and accompanied by a dog. All I was missing was the hound.

I shovelled in my last handful of potatoes, determined to get hold of a dog, some drugs, some alcohol, and enough money for a consultation with the captivating Maple. The evening would be mine—or it wouldn't be. *To adventure!*

Chihuahuas are ugly as hell, but a cross-eyed chihuahua is one long, endless hell of ugliness. Maybe that's why I chose the poor beast—out of compassion.

The lady at the other end of the leash resisted and refused to give me the mutt. *It's my daughter's, I need to keep it for her.*

She was having a hard time understanding me, so I spoke as clearly as I could. *I don't give a flying fuck.*

Being unused to meeting real charismatic punks in her tony Vieux-Montreal neighbourhood, she thought she could sweet-talk me. *But, sir...*

I negotiated the animal as the price of her not getting

punched in the face, and in the end she accepted enthusiastically.

Can I at least keep her leash?

No.

While I was at it, I took advantage of plump Mrs. Moneybags's co-operation to requisition her purse too. The poor woman was sobbing. I'm a decent guy, so I rummaged around in it, but I just kept the wallet and gave her the purse back. She thanked me without conviction. That'll teach me to be generous. But I still politely said goodbye before going on my way with my new companion.

I was almost regretting adopting the animal—it wouldn't stop yapping. I growled in its face to calm it down, but the little chickenshit pissed in my hands! I would have smashed it against a wall if I hadn't needed the urban camouflage. I dangled it in the air by a handful of fur and yelled at it. As an expert in canine psychology, I wanted to get our relationship going on a solid foundation. *I'm the boss, you little son of a bitch, and you'll piss when I say you can. Is that clear?*

Woof, it was clear.

Ghaghagha! Maple was roaring with laughter. Since she wasn't wearing a bra, all her body parts seemed to be joining in with the laughing. The masses overhanging her navel jiggled under her purple-sequinned pink camisole. She hadn't changed her outfit since the first time I'd seen her. Neither had I, as it happens. *Do you have a throat lozenge? Some guy just jizzed right at the back of my mouth.*

No, I didn't have any lozenges, but I had money.

Ghaghagha! Forty-three bucks' worth of chat, kiddo? Gonna give you my whole life story for that price. I wouldn't have wanted anything less.

Why do they call you Maple?

Her eyes dropped to her fingernails. Maybe the answer was hidden under the polish. *Because Maple spreads, kiddo. Maple spreads, get it? Haha.* She'd repeated it too many times and her laugh lacked conviction. *Going by your real name is dangerous. You should know that, kiddo.*

I knew it well, I just had to get used to it and accept that we would get to know each other from behind the shields of our pseudonyms.

Anyway, why is your dog called Sanchopanza?

Because Beethoven was already taken!

Ghahahaha! Now she was laughing genuinely, I was proud. We carried on walking.

She was swigging away from my litre of wine but didn't want any of my joint. *No soft drugs, they get me wound up.*

I took a puff to her health and pulled on the dog's leash. *Heel, minion!*

She's gotta be a girl dog, right, with a pink leash?

We shouldn't always listen to our prejudices. *I'll check later. Have you been working the streets long?*

Maple stopped short, taken aback. *Whoa, hang on there, I'm not working the streets, I'm on the sidewalk, there's a difference! I have an apartment and I'm independent, I'm a professional sex worker. I've done it all, strip clubs, call girl, government orgies, the whole nine yards! But now I work for myself. Organized crime isn't as organized as you might think, so it's more practical to organize my own stuff.*

I nearly told her about my Mafia misadventures in prison, but I held back. Women can sometimes be funny about ex-cons who've done time for murder.

Maple was lighting her fourth cigarette when she invited me to come and sit in the park. She started getting breathless in between coughing fits. *It'll be quiet there.* She licked her lips to underscore her point. I guess she was offering me a blow job out of habit. She couldn't get over the fact that I just wanted to talk to her, no cameras or documentary sob stories. *Just this? Yup, just this.* A little voice at the back of my skull, like a conscience or a psychosis, was telling me to stay close to her, to make her talk more.

For Maple, prostitution was a vocation. She didn't just do it for the money, but for love, although love was something she would never have. Incapable of submitting to a boss, passionate about alcohol, drugs, and freedom, she'd always believed that her salvation would come from one of her own human resources. She'd tried giving herself freely in the past, with no great results, so now she preferred to rent herself out. Paradoxically, that made her feel less like she was getting screwed.

Maple was sensitive, and considered emotions to have sentimental value. Since the dawn of time she'd been opening her heart and her thighs at the same time and falling in love with every horndog who showed up. Like so many others, she'd been trying to find a Greek god instead of being content with a Moroccan hustler, a bankrupt mechanic, or even a hemophiliac businessman. Then she decided to go for universal access-all-areas. It's not that she always says yes, but she never says no. So she might as well charge for it!

For a long time, she'd had tons of lovers, paying or otherwise. She offered blow jobs to every Joe Blow she saw. And when some wealthy guy was prepared to pay a premium to get intimate, she developed feelings. You can't help it; the heart's all tangled up with the body. You hook the former by occupying the latter. And she had a big heart so it was easy to stumble inside it, even accidentally.

Sometimes selling your ass is the only way to know how much you're worth. I'd still like to dance, but I'm too old. If I could save enough to get my tits redone, I could go back to pole dancing. No need to have a constant line of dicks waiting to get inside me. She paused for a moment to consult her smoke rings. *You know, random penises are pretty intrusive on a psychological level.*

A shiver ran up and down my spine. *I can imagine, but I wouldn't know.* Prison memories were penetrating me from all directions. It was time to change the subject. *You ever been hospitalized?*

Like everyone else, she'd taken a few overdoses, and as a teenager she'd tried to cut herself off from the world by opening the veins on her left arm. But the world had stitched her back up. With determination, she'd repeatedly zigzagged up and down her arteries, but in vain. She'd tried to hang herself twice, but that wasn't exactly feminine. I could identify so much with her pain; my mother had also struggled with the business of living.

I encouraged her, reminding her that some of the greatest women in the world also had the impulse for self-destruction, that she wasn't alone. Marilyn Monroe was a hysteric with nihilist tendencies, that's why women identify with her.

Maybe…

It's hard to live when you're overburdened with sensitivity or lucidity; with both at the same time it's practically impossible.

Do you think so?

I advised her to go to the library and check it out online. *It's documented with photos and moving testimonies.*

Maple was dreamy, gazing into space. *If you say so…*

On her bare arm, I noticed a messed-up tattoo with irregular lettering. *Who's Ricky?*

She stroked her biceps, tracing a finger over the name and the rose hanging over it. *Ricky's nobody, just nobody now…* She blew some smoke into her eyes to justify the tears.

Do you have any children?

She crushed the cigarette butt under her heel, grinding it again and again, as if she wanted to dig a well right there in La Fontaine Park. *Don't talk to me about my kids, I miss them so much…* Classy like Freddie Mercury, she tipped her head back to stop the tears from flowing.

I took her by one of her bony shoulders and promised her everything would be alright. I promised her so loudly that I believed it too. We were united in the same pain. *I know what it's like, if only you knew.* Poor her. And poor me.

Jesus, kiddo, you're really putting me through it! Her lighter was shaking as much as the cigarette she was trying to light. To change the subject, I offered her what was left in the bottle. She downed the remaining quarter-litre in a single swig. I like a woman who knows how to drink.

With a slap on the thigh, she gave herself the momentum to get up from our bench.

Wait, Maple, I still have more questions!

She didn't slow down; I quickened my pace.

Which police force do you work for, you fucker? Ghhaha ha… She was getting out of breath. *I need to cut down on the smoking.* As she fought back a cough, she lit herself another cigarette.

I don't work for the police, I just want to get to know you better. Can we see each other again?

She stroked my cheek gently. *Sure we can see each other again, honey! Anyway, we've been talking for more than an hour here, you owe me another thirty bucks!*

Touched that she also wanted to deepen our relationship, I grasped her hand as it rested on my cheek and gripped it in my own. *I kind of feel like you're a soul sister, Maple.*

She sprayed the park with her shrapnel laughter. *Ghaha ghahaha! Drop it with the sister thing. I could be your mother!*

6

RESTRAINT

You shouldn't abuse good things. Or women. But for very different reasons and consequences. Bébette was making me pay the price for my imprudence. She yelled and yelled at me every which way, calling me a moronic junkie, insisting we needed to go to the hospital. Obviously I resisted. It was out of the question. I might have to reveal my identity, or I might be recognized by a nurse who'd interned at Pinel. To reassure her, I tried—and failed—to stand up straight. My legs were rebelling against my central nervous system, or maybe it was the other way around. I wiped away the blood trickling out of my nose; you should always try to look presentable.

Did you snort two? You're crazy, man, those pills are for swallowing, not grinding up! And one is plenty!

In spite of my respiratory distress and the trouble I was having keeping my saliva in my mouth, I found the scene kinda romantic. Here we were hunkered down behind the dumpster of a Japanese restaurant, with my beautiful Bébette watching over me once more. She was worried about what was going to happen to me, and concern is a sign of attachment. Numbly, I felt the slaps she was giving me resonate as caresses on the drum of my cheek. They made the scenery wobble too, which created a bunch of new colours. *Fabulous!* I was seriously hallucinating. There's no denying it, chemical genius is constantly reaching new heights when it comes to creating synthetic drugs. Bravo to the biker gangs' R&D departments.

My cardiac arrhythmia was picking up speed alarmingly. It would be exaggerating to say I was afraid of dying, but it would be pretty stupid to die before I'd found my mother. From another perspective, I'd already experienced a well-lived life. Not many people can boast of having survived social services, prison, *and* psychiatric hospital. I had a child to ensure my descendance, and the *Journal de Montréal* cover for posterity. I could have left with my mind at peace, but my time hadn't come yet, no, not yet…

Keep your eyes open, for Christ's sake! Bébette had been shaking my shoulders for a long time, the sun was going to sleep and I wanted to follow its example. *You can't go to sleep before you come down! Let's go, get up, we'll go and get some free coffee at a meeting somewhere.*

Narcotics Anonymous is like Alcoholics Anonymous but with extra craziness. Instead of old drunks, it's full of high kids in varying degrees of recovery. All kinds of nutcases come together to hug each other in a church basement in between two tumbles off the wagon, it's pretty cute. But most important, at the far end of the room, a big carafe of free coffee is mounted on a pedestal. Standing with my back to the wall and a crucifix threatening to crash down on my head, I gulped down my third ration, enriched with sugar and full cream to coat my throat. I was using Bébette as a crutch. The hallucinations had stopped, but I still felt a need to hold on to something.

When it was time for the voluntary collection, Bébette

managed to steal a handful of change from the bag. *Get your coffee to go, we're heading out to eat.*

We left the survivors to their evening of prayers and other incantations and set off to find pizza.

In order to ensure my docile collaboration, Bébette promised me that we would go fuck in her luxury squat after we ate. As long as I didn't start bawling on her, of course. In spite of the trouble I was having putting one foot in front of the other, I swore to myself that I'd corral my emotions and screw her like a man.

Bébette, less of a romantic than me, didn't aspire to a long-term relationship. She had quickly learned to count her lovers on the fingers of no hands, not seeing any advantage in offering exclusive access to her ass or her feelings to just one person. Anyway, she wasn't especially sentimental. She had never felt the need to be attached and tied down, unless it was to a tree. *When the monster under your bed is your dad climbing into it, you soon learn to protect yourself.*

Lucky girl, she knew who her father was! *It's well-documented.*

With a mouth full of overcooked dough, cheese, and pepperoni, Bébette asked me to clarify what I'd said: What did you say?

I clarified. *It's documented, girls on the streets, damaged and uneducated girls were often sexually abused, just like you. It's pretty common, actually. There's an entire shelf in the psychology section in the library that might interest you, you should come with me tomorrow.*

She stole my last bit of crust and reminded me of the motto of anonymous survivors everywhere. *One day at a time,*

I was just talking about the weird attraction I felt for Maple when she appeared ahead of us, a block farther down the street. It was a sign. *Come on, let's go see her!*

Bébette didn't share my enthusiasm or my interest for the lady in question; she said Maple was a manipulative profiteer. *I've never trusted her. You have to stick a finger up her ass to feel her heart beat.*

That wounded me personally, we were going to fight if she carried on dissing Maple. *You don't really know her, she's had a shitty life too, she might be able to teach you a thing or two.*

Bébette slowed down. *I know way too much already.*

There were about a hundred metres between us and Maple when suddenly it seemed as though a light toppled over. I panicked: red and blue started flashing on the walls, dazzling the street, shredding the soft evening shadows.

Police! I was surrounded and unarmed. One car stopped at the corner of the road in front of me. Behind me, a second police car skidded to a stop with a squeal of tires. I'd been careless and had nothing to defend myself with, not even a butter knife. The overexcited police officers got out of their cars, yelling in all directions.

Don't move! Hey! Stop right there!

Dropping Bébette's hand, I moved backward, evaluating my meagre options: there were too many of them for me to fight them, and I was too rusty to shake them off if I made a run for it.

I was about to say adieu to Bébette when the biggest and burliest of the cops charged at me, barging into me with his creatine-enlarged shoulder. Bam! I landed at the entrance to a florist, although this did nothing to lessen the violence of the impact. I was waiting for the cold, metallic touch of handcuffs, the blows and the insults, but nothing. Nothing for me, at least. The action was taking place farther away, at the end of the block.

Let me go, you assholes, I haven't done anything. Jesus, I was just trying to buy cigarettes, is this a city or a dictatorship?

With one policeman holding each arm, Maple was fighting with the energy of a Bengal lion in heat. There was a lot of scratching.

I couldn't believe it. I looked all around, but not a single pig was bothering about me. They hadn't recognized me! I felt sorry for Maple, but I was relieved. They dragged her to the first cop car, doing their best to dodge her kicking and spitting, then they pushed her into the car, yelling her rights at her, and then it was over.

In less than a minute, the Montreal police had just kidnapped a woman right in front of our eyes. I was astonished. Bébette the opportunist took the chance to rub it in: *See, that woman just attracts trouble!* I didn't react to her dissing Maple, but I sped up, nervous, and incredulous that I was still free. Unbelievably, I'd somehow got away with it, just like a racist white cop with an unarmed black corpse at his feet: absolutely scot-free.

Stony McPebble had known Bébette long enough to advance her some drugs, but apparently he didn't like me at all. *I don't like you!* At least he was clear. *Your face reminds me of something, and it's not something good.*

Maybe the dealer read the newspapers. More likely he'd switched the TV on between two transactions. Anyway, I didn't want him to make the connection, so I didn't make a fuss. I tried to avoid the inquisitive stares of this paunchy guy in his forties. Even his skull, both hydrocephalic and bald, filled me with mistrust. It felt like a premonition.

His asshole face went well with his shitty attitude. He stared at me, ready to swing his fist, already clenched, at the slightest reply. I'd known nervous guys like him, both in prison and in psychiatry. I needed to either act all contrite or leap at his throat and give it my all to neutralize him. There was no room for half-measures. Violent alpha-male drug addicts can be dangerous, gangsta rap has documented this; don't fuck with Ice Cube when he's filming his family movies! For now, I was going to keep a low profile.

Bébette handled the response with dignity: *Come on, stop, it's gonna be fine. We'll share this, come on.*

Stony escorted us to the door of his building. *Don't show up here again unless you have cash!*

I'd known knives that were less piercing than his sharp stare. He was trying to intimidate me, but I didn't let myself be intimidated in front of my lover and I replied, with aplomb, *Sure!*

Bébette had four amphetamines and a finely sculpted body. All we needed was some alcohol and things would be pretty well perfect. We refined our diversion strategy as we approached a grocery store that was about to close. We had to be fast and smart.

I went in first, making sure to attract attention, muttering and lurching from one aisle to another, grumbling louder and louder. It was working, the manager and an employee were following me at an increasingly close distance, keeping watch from the ends of the aisles where I was putting on my show. I led them to the last one, pretending to search for a particular brand of chips. After a minute or two, I figured Bébette had had enough time to come in, steal a bottle of wine and leave again. Just to mix it up a bit, I insulted the two proles: *Stop spying on me, for Christ's sake, I'm not a thief!*

Taken aback, they stayed in the snack section while I went back out through the door and met up with my Bonnie one block over. She was waiting for me, her Clyde, pawing at the ground and magnificent.

Like Terry Fox, the plan had made it all the way.

There wasn't even anyone working cash when I went in, and they had all these special-offer bottles opposite the checkout!

Haha, pretty awesome! I was lit up by her phosphorescent eyes, which sparkled more than the three bottles of bubbly she'd stolen for us. With our arms full of loot, we made out right there, licking each other's tongues and already getting drunk on the idea of the drugs, alcohol, and love. Her green hair was shining in the lamplight, some festival or other was giving us a musical background, and Bébette was laughing with abandon. The night looked like being sleepless and beautiful, as beautiful as she was. Yes, being happy does bring luck.

The time to build an engine is when you have the wind in your sails. It's all about predicting nature's low blows, human nature's low blows in particular. I was dreaming hard and saving memories for a movie about my life or the movie of my death. Which would come too soon, but I didn't know that yet.

Alcohol and synthetic drugs take away your inhibitions, which is a pretty big advantage from a genital point of view. On the other hand, they also take away your inhibitions about confiding in people, which is less interesting. I was listening to Bébette anyway, who was deep in childhood reminiscences. Recklessly she even revealed that her name was Stéphanie Blanchette, and she'd escaped from East Angus, some godforsaken hole between the Estrie and the Eastern Townships. In spite of her Governor General's academic medal and her talents as a singer, she had quickly understood that real life was happening somewhere else. She'd picked up her dreads, her hopes for a better world, and headed for the city. And she was right, it was in Montreal's streets that she had discovered real life. *Life is shit.* Punks are good at summarizing. I gave her something else to think about with my tongue.

Dawn was just starting to break; we couldn't even think about going to bed. Naked on the hardwood floor, we hurt all over, but we felt good, both of us in love, even if Bébette didn't want to admit it. We stretched out our reserves of amphetamines and wine, keeping dysphoria at a distance. Unkeepable promises were flying thick and fast. She would go back to university to finish her useless visual arts certificate. As for me, I was going to become a writer and tell my story, although I'd have to sand down the edges a little: my life has been so intense people would find it hard to believe. We would become role models of success, inspirational internet influencers. The works.

And we'd have children. Bébette didn't want any but she would agree to lend me her uterus to produce a set of twins. I'd get custody of my son, and we'd move in with my mother and all of Bébette's revolutionary friends in a big squat on the Rive-Sud, a luxury commune. With my book sales, I could buy us a pad in Longueil or some other chi-chi part of town. And we'd have tons of pets: five geckos, three cats, a pony, two guard dogs, and one decorative one called Sanchopanza. Bébette started sucking me off again just to shut me up.

I needed nothing more than that to be happy: a few blow jobs a day, small amounts of drugs and alcohol, and a lot of love. What more could an honest man possibly want, except for it to last?

They say that nobody fucks like porn actresses, but that's forgetting that porn actresses are people too. Human people even, who breathe, eat, and love. And who love above all to screw and make money, let's not get caught up in altruism here. Bébette could have considered a cinematic career in the industry, she had the body and the talent for it. All she needed was to cut off her green mop, get a Brazilian, and put her hair in bunches. But she wasn't a big fan of capitalism, prostitution and its other ramifications. She was a sublime punkette, offering her natural riches graciously. If she was going to be different, might as well go all out.

Time to stop philosophizing about her situation, my two minutes were almost up. Focused on the embellishments of a stucco representation of a vine, my gaze was getting lost in the left corner of the ceiling when surprise grabbed hold of me.

Ooh…

All the while keeping the velvet warmth cocooning my rod, she was also succeeding in stimulating new nerve endings. At first it was a delicious sensation, and I thought Bébette was lingering on my testicles and then my anus with her fingertips. One fingertip, to be precise. But the roughness and frenzy of this finger made me realize that it was a tongue—and Bébette's tongue was already working away on my penis.

Sanchopanza was licking my ass! I pushed my lover away with one hand and grabbed the beast with the other. In the same movement, I sent it flying against the wall. *Pock! Woof!*

Bébette was unimpressed and started consoling the dog, which was naturally pissing all over itself. My dick and I had to satisfy ourselves, and that was distinctly less satisfactory. *Dirty bastard dog!*

It's hard to say who was more surprised to find a pair of stark-naked punks sleeping on the living room floor, the building's owner or his guests. With the dog and its turds scattered around, it must have been quite the picture. Unaware of her own incoherence, the lady with the keys to our love nest was compulsively repeating *Leave, I'm calling the police, leave, I'm calling the police!* But if we left, the police would have nothing to do there, since they don't clean up dog poop. Still, I couldn't see myself having a discussion with her about Boileau's famous line about the importance of clarity when communicating with this landlord. We got the fuck out of there.

Bébette had drifted off to sleep first, just after she made me promise I'd stay awake and swear that when she woke up we'd do some housework and leave the apartment without anyone noticing. My career as a guard was getting off to a bad start. Now I was carrying the unbearable weight of the loss of her squat. And the weight of the world on my stiff shoulders.

Sanchopanza was yapping, Bébette was muttering, and the sky was spitting at us. The kisses of the rising sun had been replaced by a drizzle shot through with cold droplets, the weather forecast was disgusting. In the middle of the afternoon, our long-suffering carcasses had nothing to eat and nowhere to go. More on edge than my knife, Bébette was grumbling endlessly. Angry at my lack of vigilance and the loss of her luxury squat, she decided to ditch me there, by the fountain in La Fontaine Park. It had to be a sign, but I couldn't see it.

On the corner of Ontario and Papineau, the sun was noticeable by its absence, as was Maple. Misery and its professional profiteers were the only ones occupying the street. Despite my total lack of attentiveness and interest, an empathetic stranger was desperate to talk to me. *We can never get past whatever is draining us from the inside.* The street worker was right, but I didn't want to hear about it just then, and I hate aphorisms. I accepted his cigarette out of politeness and went back to the park.

Sanchopanza and I played fetch with some sticks, but we quickly got fed up with it, especially him. I wandered about like a Nazgûl in pain before resigning myself to a literary salvation. I was going to take my mind off things with books and do a little research on myself: there's nothing like Google for spoiling your ego.

There was a big buzz on the internet. Going by the comments, half the country thought I was a monster and the other half was wrong. I had to hold back the onomatopoeias that wanted to come flying out of my clenched teeth, the feeds were so surprising. The library was packed, especially with families. I had to watch my language. *Darn fuckling Jebus Christmas!* Off-leash children were running around in all directions, shouting, moaning, trying to escape their parents' surveillance—parents who were convinced they were doing their job by stuffing *The Little Prince* down their kids' throats.

I gathered up a pile of newspapers and went to shelter on the top floor in a cubicle next to the music archives. Music my ass, they didn't have any rap whatsoever. They shouldn't take us for idiots.

Holy poutine, even *Le Devoir* was celebrating me! I'd become a human-interest story on a national scale. I flicked through the big titles: nothing very reassuring, they claimed to be on my trail. I stared at the picture of the Chinese woman from the convenience store, turned out she was actually Cambodian, but same same. They even had photos of the Swiss Army knife she'd stolen from me, and of the too-tight balaclava I'd had to abandon during my escape.

In all the provincial dailies, again and again, they'd chosen the least flattering of my psychiatric looks, along with some new computer-generated robot sketches, chubbier, with or without a beard or glasses, some with different haircuts. But those idiots hadn't thought of a mohawk! I was just feeling proud of my own genius when the subtitle of an article electrified my soul and took my breath away: they'd found my mother!

There was no possible mistake, the article detailed the whole case and made me overflow with joy. The Montreal police department had found my mama, the real one, not that cow in Sherbrooke. The police had taken a DNA sample from this very own mama of mine, compared it with the DNA I'd left on Wong's counter, and Bob's your uncle. Mitochondrial analysis confirmed it, I was still in the metropolis and *more dangerous than ever!* A slightly sensationalist conclusion. My own was more dignified: Mama was alive, in town, and one of these days we'd meet each other. It was documented right in front of my weeping eyes.

7

ADAPTABILITY

Gilles de la Tourette would have stayed quiet about it; I shouted, I laughed, I cursed with happiness. Sancho-panza was twirling around at the end of my joyously outstretched arms, then I pulled him back to my face and kissed him right on the mouth. *We're going to find Mama!* I was just giving him another peck when I remembered he'd been licking my ass that very morning. I stopped. But it didn't stop me from swearing with happiness. *Fuck yeah, Christ on a fucking bike, this is so fucking cool! Yeah!*

Everything was falling into place, like Russian dolls or wife-swapping. I stared at all the women I saw in the street, my mother could have been anyone. Maybe I'd even met her without realizing. Did she work the till in a convenience store, on the streets, or in the metro? We'd soon find out!

Maple would be happy to hear I was on my progenitrix's trail, knowing as she did the pain of families being ripped apart. Bébette would also be happy for me, despite her childish anger. Joy, like a meal or a genital organ, was made to be shared. I looked for both of them under the fabulous rain of this historic June, struggling to contain my happiness.

None of the parks in the neighbourhood were sheltering my lady friends. I went back down toward Rue Ontario, breaking up my journey with stops at restaurant trash cans, the opulent buffet of the destitute. Sanchopanza snacked on some leftover macaroni while I devoured dried-up sushi, lost in my deep thoughts.

A journalist's indiscretion had allowed me to learn that Mama lived in Montreal. This was a major breakthrough, but there were tons of women in their fifties living in the metropolis. How could I narrow down my search? As incongruous as it might seem for a gangster like me, I would need to enlist the help of the police.

Patience is golden. The nocturnal fauna was starting to emerge, and I was still slumped on the sidewalk, propped up in the entrance to a credit union.

I just need something to eat… I have generative muscular leukemia… Just a buck, or maybe two… A cigarette, at least…

I didn't let anyone get by me, I called out to everyone walking past.

I need to feed my dog… I didn't get my tax return back…

That worked a little better, I gathered together the thirty bucks I owed Maple, the money needed to make a couple of calls to the police, and a small surplus so I could stop by Stony McPebble's to obtain a few recreational pills for my honey and me. I hadn't actually seen her that day and I was starting to get worried. None of the anarchists or any of the other downtown good-for-nothings had seen Bébette. Had she gone off to fight the good armed fight in South America?

The police officer was less stupid than her title might have led me to believe. Despite using my most professional voice and the name of the famous journalist, which I flung around as though it were some kind of magic password, she refused to give me Mama's address. Unwilling to admit defeat, I used her full name, which hadn't been revealed in the media. *Listen, madam police officer, I understand that you're constrained by confidentiality issues, but I can guarantee you that my approach is entirely within the rules. I spoke to one of your supervisors earlier and he confirmed that you would be in a position to give me the address of Mrs. Marie-Madeleine Fontaine... Please.*

There was silence on the line. *One moment, sir, I'll put you through to the investigator in charge of the file.*

The wait seemed to go on forever, the telephone receiver weighed a ton, I was sweating with stress and hope through every pore on my body. Crammed into the phone booth, alone in the world, I was just one slick move away from getting my mother's details.

Sergeant Boutin. Who's this? Police officers are famously rude, but this one was going beyond the pale. *Who's there?*

I gave a false name and reeled off my spiel. *Mr. Detective, it's an honour to be speaking with you at last, I need some information that your superior promised me earlier in the day... We're filing a special report about the famous Pinel escapee...* You could have heard a fruit fly buzzing around.

After several seconds of eternity, he shattered the silence. *Is it you? You want to find your mother, am I right?*

I felt the world give way under my feet, the same way you might feel the world give way under your feet when you have a rope around your neck. That scoundrel! I'd thought I was about to make the kill, but I'd been the prey all along.

So, you stayed in Montreal just as I suspected. Did you read the information we let slip out today?

I could taste the salt in my sweat, it was trickling past the corners of my lips, soaking my T-shirt.

You'll never see your mother again, but we're gonna find you. Your hours are numbered. Are you still there? ... If the truth is too hard to swallow, we'll be happy to give it to you in suppository form. Can you hear me?

I was unable to articulate a single word, and anyway, what word would I have said?

Shit! With Sanchopanza under one arm, I ran for almost ten minutes, anxious to put some distance between me and the phone booth. It wasn't even that I was afraid they'd have pinpointed its location and were on their way to find me, I just wanted to get as far away from the scene of the drama as possible. They were never going to tell me where my mother was, they would probably try to hide it from me, and my presence in the city was now confirmed for them. The vice was tightening around my delicate testicles. My emotions had travelled through the Russian mountains and been abandoned to a Chechen operative. I was sick of it. I shouted *shit* a few more times for good measure.

Avoiding the main streets, I found a damp bench in a deserted park. I had to gather my thoughts. What should I do? Make a run for it? They would still end up getting their hands on me. Should I take advantage of nighttime to avoid the four-hour rush hour and cross the bridge to leave the island? It wouldn't change anything. What would I do out in the boonies? But staying where I was, just surviving and waiting, that would end my career more effectively than a mastectomy for a member of Femen. No, I was going to face this head-on, be worthy of my criminality and find my mother. Willingly or not, I didn't care how much force it took for me to get there. Fleeing is for the weak.

Now for some drugs. I needed a little pick-me-up. And something to optimize the old meningeal functioning. I pulled my cap down over my soaked mohawk, I hunched my head down into my shoulders, and I headed toward Rue Panet, Stony's place. Tucked away deep in the asshole of the neighbourhood, his building looked like shit. He must not be paying a mortgage either. Hovering somewhere between squat and outright despair, it was held together by grime. A client was leaving as I arrived, a woman from the neighbourhood, a young Haitian prostitute hooked on heroin, she was super-pretty. She had the reputation of being as hot as those sunny isles; I was hoping to buy her for myself one day. I said hi in Creole and she replied in silence. I climbed up the staircase with its urine aroma and gave a big drum roll on the trader's door. Epic fail.

Bébette was slumped on the sofa, her eyes rolling in their sockets, breasts lolling free. The big shot had stolen my little pussy!

Whadda you want? Leaving me standing in the hall, filling the door frame, Stony was guarding the drawbridge. My lover hadn't noticed my presence. Always quick to repeat himself, Stony wondered aloud again about the reasons for my presence in his abode. *Da fuck you doing here?*

Things were escalating. *I want to see my girl!*

He laughed out loud. *Hey, Bébette, is this shrimp here your boyfriend?*

Bébette stirred, looked at me with her dead eyes, then went back to smoking her cigarette. Never.

The atmosphere was heavier than a bus full of morbidly obese men.

Come on, Bébette, stop messing around!

She ignored me, totally unaware of the pain she was causing me.

Stony wasn't the sort of guy who was into physical affection. I put a hand on his shoulder, just as a gesture of politeness, so I could discuss things with my beloved. He put a fist in my face, in a gesture of total rudeness, to end the conversation. The door he slammed shut in front of me was oblivious to the blows I rained on it as I howled my lady love's name. *Bé-é-ébette!*

He must have drugged her, she didn't answer me. I thought about knocking the door down, but it would be better not to attract attention in the building. The police stay close to the rich, but they're never far away from the poor either. I could get my girlfriend later. Too bad for her.

For the first time in our relationship, Sanchopanza did his business at precisely the right moment, just outside my rival's door. Okay, so it was just a chihuahua turd, which isn't exactly going to destroy a pair of boots, but it's the intention that counts.

Fortunately, and by the grace of God, Maple was back on her street corner. *Hahaha, you're still alive?*

I gave her a hug; she grabbed my buttocks with one hand and my penis in the other.

Has anyone ever popped your cherry?

I laughed at her joke and disentangled myself from her strong grip.

Someone bust your face up? She touched the bruise on my eyebrow, assessing the damage.

It was nothing, just a disagreement. I was touched by her concern. I wanted to reserve her services before a client could show up and kidnap her company. *I have your money, Maple, thirty bucks. Can you give me another advance? I need to talk to you.*

She stared up the rainy street, first east, then west. The endless drizzle clung to our skin. The rare cars passed without slowing down. *It's a quiet night, sure we can go and chat, I'll charge you by the hour, hahahaha!*

I was going to head back to the park, but she signalled me to follow her. *It's too cold, my shift is over. I'll take you back to my place. I never do that, but you're harmless.*

Skeptical about this backhanded compliment, I followed her, honoured to be visiting her home. She offered me a cigarette and a wink, then took my shoulder. *Come on, kiddo, Maple will take care of you!*

We took five hundred detours and then we took five hundred more. Maple made us wander through half the city. *I don't want my clients knowing where I live, or the police. There are fuckers on both sides, you know!*

We walked for a long time, and I would have walked for a long time more. We moved forward side by side through the soggy night, enveloped in a cloud of our cigarette smoke and our burgeoning complicity. I was going to her home, but I had the feeling I was simply going home.

Maple lived in a basement apartment in Rosemont. *I used to live in Hochelaga, but it got rich as fuck so I left. The fucking rich, they want everything for themselves, even poor areas!* Paradoxically, her one-bedroom apartment was way nicer than I would have expected, it even had a floating wood shelf and a big black leatherette couch, barely even cracked.

Consider yourself lucky, kiddo, you're the first man who's ever been here.

I was just weighing up this luck when I froze on the spot.

Flashdance! In pride of place above the melamine table in the kitchen, there was a poster of the famous dancer draped over a chair, crowned by the movie title in big pink-and-turquoise letters. Even though they'd faded over the years, all the details of this mythical poster were familiar to me.

My mother had the same poster! It was a sign, there was no doubt about it.

Maple switched the radio on, executed an entrechat and then an arabesque before taking my hand. *Let's dance!* She pressed me against her body and then placed her hand on the small of my back. *Just follow me, baby!*

Left to right, forward, backward, I was facing ridicule and doing my best.

You move pretty good, carry on! And I followed her for another catchy song, a waltz by Mario Pelchat. *It's been so long since I danced.* At the end of the piece, she stood me in the middle of her kitchen to go and blow her nose and dry her snot. Music moves women. It's documented in *Flashdance*, among other places.

Maple also needed to talk, it's a human thing. She steeped us two Red Rose tea bags, which is a great vintage beloved by connoisseurs, and we sat down on the sofa, face to face, for a tête-à-tête. Seeing as I was the one paying, she let me begin. I started in gently by explaining the situation with my love, Bébette, who was cheating on me with Stony.

He's a mean dirty asshole, that one, I know him too. Don't worry about it, they'll soon get tired of each other. She was reassuring me, but deep down I knew this was just a secondary problem. The thing tormenting me, niggling away at me, truly obsessing my mind and twisting my soul into knots was finding my mother.

With her eyes full of pain, Maple listened to my tale for nearly two minutes before she burst into tears. *Wawawa... Your story is so beautiful, it's sad because it's fucking beautiful. And I'm not just saying that because I'm bipolar, it really touches me inside!* She wiped her face on my T-shirt and sniffed hard. I was crying too, just to keep her company. It lasted for one and a half Joe Dassin songs, us wailing in one another's arms without saying anything, with the slow dances as background music. Her skinny arms gripped me tight, cocooned me, impregnated me with real affection. I wasn't even thirsty, didn't want to get high or hit someone. We were just right like this. Maple came up for air and wiped her tears on her arm hair.

I can so fucking relate to what you're saying. I had four of them taken away from me by those fuckers at child services. They took the last two off me at the hospital as soon as they were born and there was nothing I could do about it... Waawaawaa!

Now it was my turn to let her talk about love. I took her in my arms, with my head against her chest, and I let her let it all out as I patted her on the back.

My baaaabiiieees, my little baaaabiiieees!

We were great therapy for each other. *It'll all work out, Maple, your children love you even if they don't know you. Blood doesn't lie, it's stronger than everything...*

Waawaawaa.

I couldn't even say how much time we spent like that, but at least four ballads.

If a song could change the world, John Lennon would still be alive. But songs can still do you good. We listened to the last chords of one last popular litany, we sighed in chorus, and then a car ad came on and broke the spell.

You should be a psychologist, you get all kinds of emotions out of me! Maple slapped her hands on her thighs, stood up, and headed to the fridge, Sanchopanza at her heels. *We need to celebrate that sobfest!*

She came back into the living room brandishing two big bottles of beer, more than a litre of 10% Labatts in each bottle.

I've been keeping them for a special occasion.

I was touched, I know what it takes for an alcoholic to share their stash.

Don't worry, I've still got a ton of Pabst left.

That's the advantage of getting older, you get to know yourself and learn to take care of yourself. We raised a toast to all the people we loved, even the ones we didn't know, and then we drank. And drank some more.

We were in dry dock, there was no beer left anywhere, last call at the convenience store was far behind us, and we were starting to get worried. *We're still thirsty.*

I agreed. I offered to go and get some drugs downtown, but alcohol was her favourite drug. *Anyway, you're wasted and so am I. We'll just have to make do with each other.* She tottered to the sink, rinsed her face, lit her umpteenth cigarette, and ordered me to go into the bedroom with her, giving me an unsubtle wink. *We'll give you something else to think about.*

Screwing an old whore without protection seemed risky to me. But it would also be embarrassing to ask her to lube up her pussy with disinfectant, or to refuse to give myself to such a generous woman, someone with whom I'd shared so much emotion. Trying to be positive in the face of misfortune, I followed her, reminding myself that your appetite returns when you eat, you never know until you've tried, and other such motivational expressions.

Inside every whore, there's a romantic woman—and vice versa. Logically you might have expected Maple's bedroom to be a sex dungeon littered with dirty S&M gadgets and the remains of breathless lovers, but it was actually overflowing with good taste. Bouquets of dried flowers hung over the headboard, which was itself adorned with an impressive number of trinkets. Especially cherubs and dolphins. On the wall was a triptych of black-and-white photos of children offering a rose or a kiss. High-class.

Penetrating a woman's intimacy can be disturbing. It's kind of like profaning a sacred temple, a first infiltration of the soul by immersion into her natural habitat. Maple thought I'd been watching too many documentaries and other crime shows. *It's just my bedroom, for Christ's sake. I don't get what you're going on about with your sacred stuff, you use your brain too much. Let me show you what's going on in my head!*

The engineering of the main turbines at the James Bay Project was probably inspired by Maple's powers of suction. I was amazed to find that my penis was still attached to my body after her mouth had worked on it, and it took me a few seconds to recover. She spat into a Minnie Mouse garbage can, and then lit her cigarette butt. *You came quick.*

These things are always a question of perspective. *No, you suck quick!*

Maple ended the debate by indicating that she hadn't just done it out of the goodness of her heart, she'd shown me a good time and now she wanted something in return. Saying this, she fell back on her mattress, hiked up her skirt, slipped two pillows under her pelvis, and said, *Come on, kiddo, eat me out!*

Maple had a Neapolitan pussy: gradations of brown, beige, and rose. Overlooking it, her Mount of Venus, haphazardly maintained, housed a tuft of dark, thick pubic hair, scattered with a few white ones, corkscrewing every which way the curls took them.

Where her groin met her pelvis, around a banner surrounding a disproportionately curvy heart, was tattooed the name Bruno. Maybe he was one of Ricky's friends.

Maple's mane stopped right at the top of her labia majora. Pink and plump, the clitoris's prepuce protected this masse of reddening flesh, which was already hard and reaching out to me, like the prow of a ship cutting through the oceans.

Standing out from her protruding vulva, the brown labia majora were spread by Maple, who pressed them against her thighs and exposed her vagina. The labia minora didn't really deserve their name, since they unfurled toward the outside with considerable size. They offered a very slick, light brown interior surface, where Maple's abundant wetness shone. The corolla of her labia minora was irregular, almost lacelike. The reddening flesh, swollen with desire, of the vaginal walls obstructed the way into her sanctuary. Beneath the impediment of the clitoris, the urethral meatus was also swollen, maybe because of her arousal, or maybe because of some harmless infection.

Maple revealing her genital apparatus like this allowed me to appreciate the contrast between the very pale pink—lighter even than the perineum—of the vestibule to the vagina, and the red—you could even say vermillion—of the vaginal orifice proper. In the muted light from the shell-shaped ceiling lamp, I could establish one obvious, true fact: *You have a very beautiful pussy, Maple.* Women love getting compliments, it makes them feel kindly toward you.

Whole calendars had been torn off the wall since the last time I'd kissed a vagina on the mouth. The taste of the smells reminded me of the breeze at the edge of a river, and breaded lobster, and the crumbs at the bottom of a bag of salt-and-vinegar chips, and the bitterness of long-steeped tea, and black liquorice too.

Numbed by the alcohol, it took Maple an eternity and a quarter to come. *Aaaahrarahahrah yes!*

It's incredible how laughter, crying, and orgasmic yelps are all in the same register. My tongue couldn't take it anymore, nor could I. I could look forward to torticollis the next day, but you have to live in the present. Maple rewarded me for my efforts by inviting me to rest my head on her chest. Her breasts were actually a little farther down than her chest, but her chest was still pretty nice. With her plastic fingernails, she scratched my back, stroked my hair, and hummed some classical music: "Total Eclipse of the Heart."

I woke up a long time before I was able to open my eyes. My mouth was pastier than peanut butter frosting, my skull wanted to split, and all my muscles hated me. I would have offered my kingdom for a glass of water, but I wasn't the knight ready to get up to go get it. In the time it took to sort out my ideas, I had remembered where I was. Through the thin slot I could part my eyelids, a lavender bag and some dried carnations confirmed that I was in Maple's bed. I'd have preferred to be in Bébette's arms.

A heat wave was burning under the sheets. Maple must have been going through morning menopause. Despite my body's utter sloth, my head was happy. My friend snoring at my side, I was hidden away, safe from the long arm of the law, and the sun was peeping through the blinds with a generous light. It was going to be a beautiful day.

We had a lie-in, spooning until past noon. Maple woke up now and then, but I helped her fall back to sleep by singing "Sweet Painted Lady." I watched over her as she slept peacefully. I couldn't have known that a violent death was preparing to slaughter me, such is the furious épée of fate.

Despite the vacuity of our lives and the ineluctability of our deaths, we have to cling on to our dreams, by their guts if necessary. Sleepy, dreamy, I fantasized about leaving with Maple and Bébette in a big convertible Jeep, picking up my mother along the way, and crossing borders at 150 kilometres an hour. We would go to Mexico, Peru, or some other country where it would cost next to nothing to buy ourselves a duplex by the sea, open a pizzeria, or smuggle drugs. I must have been imagining the pizzeria a bit too hard; hunger ended up waking up Maple.

Watching her wake up, I noticed another tattoo, this one between her shoulder blades: *I love Richard*. I'm curious—and curiosity is a sign of intelligence. *Is that the same Ricky?*

She shrugged. *No, Richard's worse than Ricky, stop asking me questions.*

My gaze was caught by the small of her back. Another one! Here was written *Manon 4 ever*. This woman had definitely loved a lot.

Since her makeup had more or less deserted her face, she got up to go and remove the remaining crud. I used some butts in the ashtray to roll my first cigarette of the day. I politely waited for my companion before I lit up. I dropped the smoke on the kitchen lino when I saw her coming out of the bathroom, no makeup, completely natural. She didn't look like herself at all. With her hair tied back, her face fresh, she was a beautiful woman. And a beautiful woman that I knew, it was obvious now. When masks drop, truth is revealed.

Maple, I swear, our paths have crossed in another life. She didn't believe in reincarnation, she thought I was a bit too into the esoteric stuff. But I felt in my gut that our paths had been braided together, one around the other, at some time or in a dimension we couldn't put our finger on. *Come on, Maple, the whole fucking gang can't be wrong, Hindus, Buddhists, even Jesus got reincarnated not long after he was executed. Do you really not believe in anything?*

Maple stirred the scrambled eggs she was making us, before concluding practically, *I believe in the holy face of the queen, and in Mackenzie King's face too. The only miracles in my life are the two or three times little Robbie Borden's appeared to me on a hundred-dollar bill. That's all, nothing to get down on your knees for, or at least not to God.*

The eggs were salty. *Salt's my favourite spice.* She would have offered me toast or a glass of juice, but the fridge was basically empty except for eggs, a ton of eggs. They were on deep discount at Super C. *And they're full of protein.* She agreed to let me waste one on spiking up my mohawk. You can leave it up to the whims of the season if you want, but a proud punk wears his crest in the air.

What's your plan for the future, I mean short-term?

I only had one and a half goals: finding my mother, and Bébette, if she would agree.

Professionally speaking, I mean. You've got nothing to smoke and nowhere to go. What are you gonna do now, go and beg on Saint-Denis?

That option was too risky now, with the pigs in uniform on my trail, it wasn't a good idea to linger in busy streets. I admitted I had no idea where my next dollar was coming from. My professional ambition was more stagnant than bayou water. Anyway, like Dinosaur Jr. sang, When I want something, I don't want to pay for it, I walk right through the door.

I strategically hit the puck back to her. *Can you help me? Are you a careers advisor?*

She stopped picking her teeth with the fork, placed it on the table, sniffed solemnly, and expounded her idea to me. *You can work for me and I'll work for you. We'll be a team!* The confusion contorting my facial muscles made her laugh. *Rahahaha! Trust me, it's a fucking amazing idea. You're gonna be my pimp!*

You're gonna be my whore?

She preferred the term hooker, it sounded more European, more classy. *But basically, yes! You have to make money with your ass before time wrecks the inventory. The pigs are after me, they won't leave me alone. You could scout around while I'm drumming up business. Then you can let the clients see you, let them know I have protection. And most of all you can help me manage logistics. Next week's the Grand Prix, the biggest pussy-for-hire market in all of North America, the godsend of the year. Fat wallets roll into town, it could be our ticket to big bucks!*

Her enthusiasm was contagious, I could already see the line of queens with their Ferrari ginches and their own-brand rubbers from the drugstore down the street. With her powerful suction, Maple could drain half a dozen dicks an hour, no sweat! I still didn't know how I was going to manage to find my mother, but while I waited I needed to eat well, drink, and get high. This would give me a steady job as well as the money to carry out my search.

I'd already jumped with both feet into this entrepreneurial project, but, a freemason through and through, I wanted to reassure myself about the solidity of the business plan. *It's an interesting idea, but how much do I get per trick? It's pretty risky, ya gotta admit.*

Her finger, yellowed from cigarettes, wagged from left to right. *Nonono, you're not risking anything, you'll be working in the shadows. I'll give you ten bucks per client, whether it's a blow job or taking it up the ass. Plus you get food and lodging, with eggs or whatever there is. Take it or leave it.*

She was a great negotiator, she wasn't leaving me much room to manoeuvre. But I still had to get her to move a little, just for form's sake. *Okay, but I get to sleep on the left side of the bed.*

The cracked nail varnish wagged again. *Nonono, you'll be sleeping on the couch, except when I feel like having you.*

I shrugged. At least I'd got her to state the clauses of the agreement. *It's a deal!* Fate is unpredictable: this exceptional woman, unknown to me just a few days earlier, was now my mistress, my best friend, and my business partner. We sealed our agreement with a firm handshake. Montreal would soon be seeing its first punk pimp.

8

COURAGE

Victoria's Secret is that she doesn't wear any underwear. *No, it's a hard no!* Lingerie is for show, not for practising whores. Maple was insistent, but it was my job as the responsible procurer to watch over the budget.

Let's at least get some black underwear from Walmart, we'll charge extra if the client wants to rip them, but no lace! Maple stayed planted in front of the window, dreamily admiring the crotches of the wooden mannequins. *Look how cute they are, with the purple hearts and the frills.*

I took her by the arm. *Come on, you're making yourself suffer for no reason. You've been standing on the sidewalk for three days and we don't even have enough money to get decent groceries. Before we put hearts on your frills, we need to put food on the table!*

I had to distract her fast. Maple was starting to whine, which signalled an incoming tantrum. A week of hanging out together had been enough to show me her mood swings. She could start crying or burst into laughter at the drop of a hat, or even less. Once she'd got going, anything went: insults, threats, tears, then promises and hugs. She was a child. I had to console her every time. Our relationship was starting to get worryingly parental.

From another perspective, with everything she had to hold in and swallow every day, I could understand how she felt. And that was without even taking into account the occupational annoyances and attacks. We shouldn't be surprised that distress seeks relief even if we try to sweep everything under the carpet. As the good prince, I endured her crises and comforted her, promising her a whole bunch of garters as soon as we made some big bucks.

She was very professional, always snapping back to normal as soon as a potential dick rocked up. Through flair and experience, she could smell them coming a hundred paces away. Immediately, she stopped her tantrums, set her face into her femme fatale mask, and swayed her hips. Poking her tongue out slightly between each word, she stalked her prey. *Hahahaha, you've finally found lurve, you lucky gold-seeker...* That was her favourite line. As soon as she spotted a fish, she cast out into the middle of the street, right into the traffic, hoping it would bite. They bit less than we'd hoped. The regulars were saving up for the Grand Prix, and Maple was facing some fierce competition.

People offer way more supply than there is demand. Just in our block alone, we had all genres of genders: dick or no dick, breasts or no breasts, some with male and female equipment plus new boobies that cost five thousand bucks for the pair. That's not even mentioning the newbies, and the Crips' and Bloods' girlfriends and groupies, freshly released from care homes for the summer season. Deeply motivated and with the energy of youth, some of them could work as many as a dozen clients a day, without counting their lovers and other associates. Unfair competition.

Maple's stats weren't so impressive, averaging barely four dicks a day. And she had to go out and curb-crawl right into the street, agree to discounts, extras, and promise strong emotions. I could help be convincing in that department. Having known the vacuum in question, I could give it an enthusiastic recommendation. However, as far as possible, I avoided coming into contact with the clients. They were disreputable people, literally unclean—and figuratively too.

To be honest, I was believing less and less in our business. Even with overseeing the surveillance at a distance, and even though the pigs were pretty complicit in the tourist attraction of prostitution, I felt vulnerable, pointlessly exposed. And above all, I had to endure wasted hours on the sidewalk for a measly hundred dollars. Barely a drop of jism in the ocean. Deducting the cost of my new switchblade, my cigarettes, alcohol, pills, and poutine, I had fifteen bucks left in my pocket. Fifteen fifty, to be precise. Not exactly enough to buy a sports car and some assault guns to accomplish my mission.

People listen to Céline more than they read her. That wasn't what my target was expecting me to say. She moved away, intimidated. It's a pretty funny joke for people who have a certain type of cultural baggage. And I assumed this taciturn brunette had cultural baggage. She was wearing a suit and carrying an armful of books. And the icing on the cake: she was looking through the French novels section—my favourite. It was a sign.

I've read some interesting works written by the few African men of letters, or by the rare intellectuals from South American juntas, or from the Chinese dynasty, but French authors are the sine qua non, the absolute crème de la crème of writers. I'm talking French from France, obviously, not our own muddy little backwater or the masturbatory autofiction our writers produce. Go French literature or go home—and do it good and hard like the Marquis de Sade.

I applied a little saliva to my crest and moved closer to the brunette, studying the shelves close to her. Like a cheetah ready to pounce, I was waiting for her to pick up a book so I could show off my learning again. Finally she took hold of one.

I pounced. *Did you know, Perec managed to write an entire novel without using the letter E? Without putting anything interesting in it too, as it happens. It's deathly dull. I forced myself to read fifty pages looking for the famous missing letter. I got fed up pretty quickly, or should I say quicklee.*

She was in complete control of herself and didn't laugh. But she did put down Georgie Porgie's massive tome. Docile, just the way I like them. She was ranking pretty highly in my scoring system.

We were solidly flirting. I was just gearing up to invite her to the toilets on the lower floor in order to take our relationship to the next level. I felt some guilt, since I was already involved with Bébette, and with Maple in a way. But I wasn't being unfaithful. On the contrary—I was being faithful to myself: I like diversity.

If I might allow myself to make a suggestion, you should come back this way, toward Victor Hugo. He wipes the floor with the whole damn lot of them! This good gentleman wrote essays, novels, and poetry. How did he ever find the time to be an alcoholic? Pretty impressive, right?

She took a step back. *Yeah, thanks, I know, I teach literature at the university.*

Boom! This was in the bag. When women start revealing the details of their professional lives, their G-strings are basically already around their ankles. *I'm a serious fucking fan of French literature, it's so great to meet you! You must have a lot to teach me!*

A few more steps back, a nervous laugh, and she turned on her heel.

Wait for me, we need to talk, we have so many things in common!

I raced down the stairs after her, planning to meet her at the checkout counter when I saw my own face.

That damn skinny mug, I was starting to get fed up with it,

fed up to the back teeth, the front teeth, and all the other teeth. It's not that I'm lacking in ego, but the media were really going overboard on my case. I get that their interns don't have anything to cover during the summer, but still, making the front page twice in one week? I abandoned my beloved at the checkout desk and snatched up the rag. *A Murderer in Our Streets!*

Seriously? Was this an ad for a Tarantino movie or a serious newspaper article?

Although recognized not criminally responsible blah blah blah, *nicknamed "Mama's Boy" and sometimes "the Beast"* blah blah, *two murders and the same number of attempted murders to his name* blah blah *aggravated rape* blah blah *the minister of justice is in hot water and* blah blah *legal project to make collection of saliva routine* blah blah *confirmation following the analysis of samples taken from his mother…* Mama! …*mitochondrial DNA of the assassin sent to Quebec's forensic analysis lab.*

He who says analysis says file. He who says file says information about my mother. He who says information about my mother says get out of my way. Hold my beer, I'm coming in.

You can't leave me, kiddo, we're a team!

Maple, predictably, was taking it personally. She raised her hands; I raised my guard. With her, it was always hard to tell if she was going to hit me or hug me.

Waawaawaa! She started fake crying, pulling out tufts of hair. *Everybody always dumps me!* Nuance was an alien concept to her. *Nobody loves me, waa!*

On the burning sidewalk, I sat down next to her, stroked her thigh, and reassured her. *You know, in the end we all die alone, isolated, with our secrets, our hurts, and our regrets. It's not just you going through this, every single person in the world is condemned to the same cruel fate, it's just the way it is.* Finally I was finding a use for all my existentialist reading.

But I don't want that, I want to be loved! Maple pressed herself against me like an exhausted kid, begging me to stay with her. It made me feel needed, but I had to find my mother.

I have a chance to find her, in Quebec. But she's kind of a prisoner of the system. I need to go down there, I might need to fight, or kill some bad guys. It's risky.

Her eyes sparkled. I represented the knight hero of all the books she'd never read. *You really love her, it's so beautiful!*

Heroism suited me, that's a fact. *It's beautiful, but it's dangerous. I need to find some kind of cash cow that pays better than you so I can buy a gun and a car.*

I wanna come with you! I have family in Quebec too! I'll work my ass off, I'll suck enough guys off to buy us a return ticket! Come on!

She wanted it so much she almost managed to convince me. With the money coming in from the Grand Prix, anything was possible. With a heart full of friendship for Maple and love for my mother, I said yes. *Yes!*

Maple yelled with joy. *I knew we'd stay together! Okay, kiddo, we're gonna work like crazy all week, we're gonna be serious about this, but at night we'll party! Jesus, Quebec City! It's twenty years since I set foot in that shithole, we have to celebrate!*

I had a feeling Epicurus had written some quote saying the same thing. I'd look it up later. *You're right, beautiful Maple, let's celebrate this!*

Maple and I clung to each other as we tottered along. Her balance was more precarious than a career in the arts. In fact, we were holding each other up so we didn't melt right there on the sidewalk. The purpose of our walk was simply to palliate the negative effects of our respective blood alcohol levels by ingesting massive doses of cocaine. Hence our unsteady stagger toward Stony's apartment. My little inner voice was yelling at me not to go, but the big voice of pleasure—inhibitions flung to the winds after multiple litres of cheap wine—was whispering to me to keep going. *Everyone this way!*

Bébette opened the door. *Beeeebeeette, you're so beautiful.* I fell into her arms and invited myself into the apartment. *Hiii, Stony!*

His eyes were wider than a pair of toonies; he couldn't believe it. He would have leapt at my throat if he hadn't had his hands full. Stony was cooking up his favourite freebase recipe with a flame from a full-on blowtorch. And he wasn't doing it on the spoon like some small-time addict, no, not him, he was cooking crack on a spatula!

I gotta tell ya, Stoneee, and it'sh not because I've been drinking, no wayyy—you're an admirable man. We could be good friendsh. Right then I was bubblier than the frothing crack.

I'm gonna kill that fucker, I'm gonna fuckin' kill him.

Hold on, we have cash! Super-Maple flew to my rescue. Numbers are a universal language that always make themselves understood, even with people who aren't on the same wavelength.

Stony put down the spatula and the crusted powder on the living room table, among the cans, ashtrays, leftover kebabs, and a syringe. Then he turned off the blowtorch, which reassured me, given his legendary predilection for using makeshift weapons to manage his conflicts. To lighten the atmosphere, I hummed a bit of Drake's "Back 2 Revenge."

Shut your mouth! Christ, Maple, who is this fucking shrimp you've picked up?

I thought about ripping his face off, but I wasn't in any condition to do that. Loyal to the core, my lady friend advised him to mind his own business and give us a gram and a half of Colombian spices. While they were doing business, I took the opportunity to make eyes at Bébette, who was unreceptive.

It was a rare night that Maple wore a bra, but she made the most of it by hiding the baggie in it. She was an expert at manoeuvring, she helped me move away from the wall, the handy support device I was leaning against. *Come on, kiddo, let's go home.*

Maybe out of jealousy, or to impress Bébette and win her heart back, or just out of sheer bravado, I allowed myself one last jibe before I left: *Bald guys can't get it up!*

This was too much for Stony. Like a blind man in an orgy, I didn't see anything coming, but I certainly felt it. He must have jumped up behind me and punched me in the back in the same move. I was thrown out into the filthy corridor and crashed into a wall. My forehead took the brunt of the impact, right on my target, bang!

I turned around with a crushing retort on my lips, but he interrupted me by smashing his smooth skull into my teeth. *Crunch!* Blood immediately started trickling down my chin and my throat. And then I swallowed a tooth, which scratched my trachea on its way down. *No way, you fucking piefe of ffhit, you've broken my new tooth! Jevuff, and it waf a nife new tooth all paid for by the government...*

Maple escorted me out of the building before washing my face with my own sweater. Every reason for drinking is a good one, but this one was really something. Getting your face smashed in makes you thirsty. Even Maple was thirsty, which just goes to show what an empathetic woman she was. *But where can we get fomething to drink at thif time of day?* My lady of the night led me to Pink Tiger, a Vietnamese den where they served duck fetuses and discount alcohol. She knew one of the people there trying to get a visa, very personally.

I'm the only one who'll agree to use egg noodles without charging extra.

That damn Maple, she specialized in everything. *Okay, I fee…*

With a bottle of strong alcohol under our arms, tucked up in our armpits, we headed back to the apartment. Both my lip and my bitterness were growing visibly. Stony was going to pay for this, I was planning on exacting vengeance, in the therapeutic meaning of the word, as soon as I could. But murdering such a notorious coprophage risked drawing the cops' attention to my honey and me. It's a hard life, being a killer on the run, I'd have to wait. Given time, things would work themselves into the right position, like a knife between two vertebrae.

The patron saint of amputees interceded on my behalf. The mixture of Vietnamese alcohol and cocaine had made my bile rise, which turned out to be a pretty useful nausea: I found the shard of my tooth on the surface of my barf. Maple played dentist with a tube of superglue. Even though the tooth was a little out of position, it was barely noticeable, and my manly voice returned. *Thankf, Maple, thankf a lot!*

Night was succumbing to day. In the dysphoric aurora, we froze in time. Our genitals were irritated, our paranoia amped up to the max. Dust floated around our heads. We took it in turns to get up and peer out through the blinds, reassuring ourselves there was nothing going on outside, nothing except real life, taxpayers driving around in their cars and the discordant song of all the birds in full throat. The purplish suitcases under our red eyes contained the corpse of the coming day. It was too late to do anything worthwhile with it. We had to wait for the sun to rise and our downer to set.

Gonna be a long day. Maple was stretching out our last beer as she rolled and unrolled our last bill, the one we'd used to snort our last line. *We've only got two smokes left.* She wasn't even answering me anymore, subsumed as she was with the distress experienced by everyone coming down. That famous guy Khabibi Gibran put it very well in Arabic: *You pay with pain in the crucible of your fun.* No getting away from it.

I'm going out for a walk, okay? Like cat hair on a black shirt, anxiety was sticking to everything. Hunched over, fists clenched, Maple made me want to help her, but distress is personal.

You okay, Maple? I wanna let you rest for a while. We overdid it yesterday. Try to sleep. I'm just going to the library and then I'll come back. Want me to bring you something by Christiane F. or Nelly Arcan?

Anguish dried the words on her lips. But she signalled to me with a shake of her head, a head that I stroked with my fingertips. She didn't want anything.

I'll be quick, I'm gonna take care of you.

I saw her eyes fill, it was too much for everyone, I left her apartment without looking back.

It's always hard to come back to reality. It wasn't just my sandpaper tongue and my lead feet that weighed me down, the atmosphere was heavy too, the sky was low, the city was dirty. It was a day for staying in bed, but Maple struggled with comedowns and was draining the little energy I had. It was better to go out and get some fresh air, beg some money, find some cigarettes, and go get some books to take my mind off things. It was ages since

I'd stolen anything by Emil Cioran, that would perk me up a bit.

I'd barely left the block, flicking my eyes left and right so I could spot the cops, when I noticed the police on my right. A patrol car was stopped, hidden behind a cedar hedge two hundred metres away. Were they lying in wait for my employee? For me? I wasn't about to give them the chance to tell me.

Standing still on the sidewalk, trying to look nonchalant, I stared at the building on the other side of the street, but I kept the car in my field of vision with a furtive eye. I pretended to stretch, the car's headlights turned on, and the cops started the engine. That was my signal to leave. My face was seriously messed up, but my calf muscles and my desire for freedom were in great shape.

I took to my heels, heading left; they stepped on the gas, drove up behind me, but didn't set the sirens going. I climbed a metal fence and cut between two buildings, hung a right, ran at full tilt across a parking lot, popped out on a road I didn't know, slipped in between two triplexes, and hid behind a bush. And I waited.

I waited for a long time, in vain. The girl cop had taken a different road and hadn't radioed for backup. I'd moved too fast, I couldn't tell whether they'd identified me, whether they were spying on me so they could catch me, if they were just there by chance, or if they were planning to shoot on sight. A thousand scenarios flashed across the screen of my panic. It's hard to know if you're just being paranoid when you have excellent reasons to worry.

I wet my head at a house with no guard dog, flattened my hawk, manoeuvred my cap down over my swollen tattoo and set off again, incognito. I headed downtown, lost in thought, when the evidence suddenly jumped out at me. I needed to dump Maple, she was just dead weight, the corpse of a vanishing twin holding me back. A twin that I loved, a friend, a business partner, but a millstone and a risk nonetheless. She would have to get me the cash to buy a gun and a car in the next week or I'd leave her. I'd made my decision. Every self-respecting pimp has to look out for his own interests first.

Hunger was floating in the bile of the bad wine, twisting my guts. Close to downtown, I took up a post at the entrance to a Subway, determined to get someone to give me a sandwich full of MSG. *Hello, ma'am, would you care to buy me a little six-inch?*

I opened the door for everyone without discriminating. And anyway, I'm not sexist or racist, I'm very equal opportunities in my contempt. *Hello, sir, please don't hesitate to get one for me too. Ranch sauce please!*

Nobody was really biting, and I was just about to say screw it to the whole thing and go dumpster diving when my flamboyant Amazon got off a bus nearby.

Bébette was wearing new tights, purple, freshly ripped, and a placard. I abandoned my career as a porter and crossed the road, yelling her name. She waited for me on the sidewalk, with her pointless anti-globalization sign over her shoulder.

Hi!

Hello! She clasped me in her arms, full of compassion but empty of love. Love gets used up; it can still give head, but whatever. I could sense she no longer felt anything much for me. *Sorry about yesterday, you were asking for trouble but you didn't deserve that.*

Always the tease, I laid it on thick. *Poor Stony, the truth can be shocking!*

She gave a fake smile. *Anyway, give it a rest with saying I'm your girlfriend. I'm nobody's girlfriend.* She started walking north and I followed, trying to save the furniture from the burning building of our love.

That's not something you just get to decide unilaterally. With everything we've been through together, you are my girlfriend in a way.

Nope, not your girlfriend. We got high together two or three nights, that's all. We're just friends. And speaking as a friend, here's a piece of advice: stay away from Maple, she's a whole bundle of trouble.

Now she was showing her hand and letting the pussy out of the bag. *You're jealous! You're jealous of Maple! Come on, she's not my girl, she's my whore!*

Bébette was more obstinate than a feminist lady politician. She stopped dead and pointed her finger right in my face. *Never call a woman a whore, never! And if anyone's getting screwed here, it's you!*

Confused, sad, and feeling other related emotions, I watched her and her righteousness march off. Had our wonderful bond evaporated just like that? Yup. Nothing lasts forever, not even Dirk Diggler. I started meditating on the meaning of existence in a world where all hope of building a relationship over the course of time is pointless and exhausting, but I cut it short. I was starving. I went off to rummage in a restaurant dumpster so I could eat my emotions.

The sun was setting over the city. Between the end of a loony-left demonstration and the launch of yet another music festival, the city fauna mingled in its hot stomach, the metropolis's guts were grumbling. Emilie Gamelin Park was home to more exotic creatures than the Granby Zoo could ever imprison. Festivalgoers in their hundreds dissolved into the crowd of punks, druggies, and the other usual suspects. The subway kept spitting out continuous waves of nobodies. People of all colours, all smells, and for all tastes. I was taking advantage of the crowds to do a bit of frotting when I spotted the perfect target: an overloaded Asian pack horse.

I approached the Korean with the Kodak from behind. He was aiming and shooting at his two fellow travellers, who were of indeterminate sex and wearing women's clothes. These models were holding their poses, plastering on their radiant smiles and their victory signs for every snap. The models' purses dangled from the patriarch's shoulders, weighing him down on one side, but a chic fanny pack attached to his belt kept him balanced. This reeked of the emerging economy: the nouveau riche ready to get fleeced by my careful attentions.

No, no thanks. He didn't want to let me sweet-talk him, nor entrust me with his camera.

I will prendre la picture, you can trust me!
No thanks!

I could see his muses were starting to get worried, a few metres away from us.

Yes, for fuck's sake, I said yes, give me the camera!

A vulture sank its claws into my shoulder, but when I looked behind me it turned out to be a pig's trotter.

Are you okay, sir? This man giving you any trouble?

The Korean shook his head so vigorously it looked like he was going to screw it right off. *No no, thanks, no no.*

He'd been pretty consistent through this whole interaction. My cardiac arrythmia settled down when the police officer let go and advised me to get out of the park. I wasn't taking any chances. I answered in English: *Yes, sir!*

From the sidewalk opposite, I continued to observe my prey. The Korean guy must have filled up three memory cards just taking pictures of buildings. Maybe he was an architect. I waited patiently, begging for a few coins to save face, as Sartre, a famously ugly French psychiatrist, might have said. After he'd photographed everything possible in the way of buildings, protestors, and lampposts, my little Samsung representative led what must have been his wife and mother, or his sister and daughter, into the walking crowd. Unaware of the neighbourhood, they were heading east, to the gay village and its endless garlands of horrible pink balls.

My work ethic was in conflict with the lure of profit. The city was overflowing with potential clients, I should have been out hustling my trick-turning chick, but I could sense that all the potential marks would only bring in small change. I decided to gamble everything on the Tokyo stock exchange and stick with my Kodak family.

Plunging into the flow of pedestrians myself, I left a little distance between me and my quarry. A distance that was pretty hard to maintain, given that they kept stopping to immortalize the scene every block. And Sanchopanza kept yapping heart-rendingly every time I tried to put him on the ground. I checked all around me to make sure no police officers had clocked my little game, and then I carried on tailing my mark.

I'm such a good sleuth, I stayed on their tail right into enemy territory. The things we do for money! I avoided making eye contact with any of the bears and beefcakes as best I could. But Sanchopanza was gaining in popularity the deeper we penetrated into the village, and it was getting pretty tricky fending off the advances of all these hunks wanting to pet my dog while I attempted to keep my prey in my crosshairs. I'm a resourceful guy though, so I managed to follow them all the way to safety. Safety in this case was a residential cross street that led down to the big brown taxpayer-subsidized Bell Tower.

My prey probably hadn't listened to the radio, so they would have been unaware of a dangerous, yet noble and courageous, predator in the streets of the metropolis—in other words, me. Anyway, they probably wouldn't have understood the French even if they had listened to the radio. They didn't know what they were missing by not speaking my beautiful, historic language, redolent of music, the scent of herbs, goat cheese, and baguette.

One of the women was getting impatient as the man rummaged through his fanny pack. This was more than a bonus, this was winning the jackpot: he was searching for the keys to their rental car. I was going to fill up my coffers and get myself a set of wheels in one lucky streak. Wisely, I chose to let the guy find his keys before I swooped down on him like a screaming eagle. As soon as he held up the bunch, I left my spy post, a bush, and raced toward them, knife in hand. *This is un holdup! Give me your clés and your argent!* I had to act fast, there were some festivalgoers in the street, I could already hear their voices.

No no, thanks!

I snatched the keys out of his hand. *Ain't no "no thanks," fucker, give me your purse, and you too, you crazy fucker, give give! Oh, Jesus fuck!* Some have-a-go hero came racing up with his clique behind me. I didn't have any time to lose, I shut myself in the car with my chihuahua, a purse, a fanny pack, and a great whoosh of adrenaline.

Jesus, it was a standard! I stalled on the first try. The second too. It had been years since I'd driven this kind of aberration, I had some problems doing parallel manoeuvres without stalling the engine. Especially with the panicked shouts of the Koreans and the queen in his lacy violet tank attempting to smash the window with his elbow, no doubt trying to impress his little gang of gays.

Vvvvvrrrmmm, ciao, jerks! Luckily I can keep a cool head. Off I went!

I was sweating, and my heart was in "imminent infarctus" mode, but I was happy. Okay, happy but stressed. I was panting, trying to catch my breath and ease the stabbing pain in my rib cage: I had a side cramp like old Benny Johnson's before he got caught for doping. What a race! Without a doubt, I'd just accomplished the equivalent of a marathon at a full sprint.

Leaving the crime scene would have been the logical thing to do, but I couldn't figure out how to change gears, and the ruckus had inevitably alerted the police. No doubt those fuckers who'd tried to block my getaway had given my description and the licence plate number to the cops. I'd be a sitting target for the first patrol car I passed. So I abandoned the wheels at a gas station and continued on foot, with my purse and my fanny pack.

A punk carrying a purse gets some funny looks. I made a second stop behind a church to check out the swag. Red Rackham couldn't have hoped for better treasure: some hundreds, some fifties, and then some twenties. Tons of them! I'd hit the jackpot here. The tourists must have just arrived in the country, I'd lightened them of their load before they could spend their holiday cash. Without taking the time to count it, I filled my pockets, my socks, my underwear, and carried on running even faster.

Rosemont's a long way from downtown. But I ran without stopping, I was running toward my destiny, carried on the wings of wealth.

The pain in my side had eased off, I could breathe without gasping, but I stayed crouching by the apartment door for another ten minutes. Despite all the detours and red herrings I'd taken, I was afraid the police had followed me, that they were about to bang on the door or knock it down. And maybe the afternoon's pigs were still at the end of the road just waiting for backup. I preferred to wait as I counted up the juicy fruits of my labour.

Enough time had passed since I'd got back, I could relax. Or at least relax as far as the galvanizing excitement allowed, letting my dreams run away with me. I was rich, I had nearly two thousand bucks in my pocket! Every day, and on every continent, people kill for less than that.

I was so sure Maple was out streetwalking by herself that I broke the silence by whistling one of Bon Jovi's sonatas. I drank a glass of water, then another, and then another. I was looking forward to seeing Maple and sending her out to get us a bottle of luxury wine at the depanneur, maybe even something with a cork, very fancy. Our trip to Quebec City was becoming a reality; now, that called for a sip of red.

But then I had a moment of doubt. I remembered Bébette's warning and I wavered. What problems could Maple cause me? Could she stop me from finding my mama? Was she really out working right now or had she recognized me and was she in the local police station denouncing me at this very moment? No, she was a kindred soul, we'd been friends for a few days now, she wouldn't betray me. I was struggling to believe myself, worry was winning me over, but I tried to put things in perspective. And when I went to take a piss, I almost pissed on myself.

Jesus, what are you doing here? Stretched out naked in the bottom of the bathtub, holding a razor blade, she started whimpering. *I thought you'd dumped me, that even you didn't want me anymore.* Here, Freud and his interns might have made a link with the key moments in my childhood, but when I saw her in the bath, about to slice open her veins, it rang a loud bell in my subconscious and in my conscious as well.

Nooooooo, don't do it! I launched myself at her, grabbed the blade out of her hands, cutting my thumb in the process, grabbed her by the hair, and pulled her out of the bathroom without ceremony, opening the doors with her head.

The unmade bed caught her mid-flight. She screamed in panic. *Stop, stop, I'm sorry!*

I saw black, and then red, and then nothing. When I came round, I was straddled on top of her, with my fist raised, at the point of no return. I have no idea what incomprehensible clinical subconscious psychosomatic transferral had possessed me, but I was about to hit my friend.

Don't hit me, please!

I was frightening myself. In spite of my bleeding hand, I grabbed her face and kissed it all over, with my lips and my tongue, on her mouth, her forehead, her eyes. I'm sorry! And I cried all over her, all over the bed, about everything in my life. It was worse than when I was with Bébette, I was whining and squalling, unable to stop.

Maple trembled to begin with; she was terrified. But after a few minutes she understood and stroked my head, patted my back. *Go on, kiddo, have a good cry, it'll make you feel better.*

Two thousand bucks? Christ, that's easily enough to get a gun, a car, and find your mother! Maple couldn't get over it, all these new banknotes, still beautiful despite their sojourn inside my tighty-whities, spread out on the melamine table, all the queens heads up.

Jesus, money is so beautiful! People can say what they wanna say, those fancy museum types, but good money lined up nice is some serious art! Through our cigarette smoke, her eyes glowed like a thousand forest fires.

If everything goes well, we can all move in together!

She jumped into my arms. *You're the greatest, you're the best, you're the fucking shit! I love you! I'm such a jerk, thinking you'd abandoned me, sorry again, you don't deserve me.* She was a pretty intense lady.

To change the subject, I opened two cans of beer. I didn't want to return to my watery outpourings of the previous day. I was worried I was losing my stoicism, getting emotional. I guess my years in psychiatry are responsible for that little weakness, but still, a man should know how to hold it together, he can't go bursting into tears in a whore's arms for every yes or no. I popped my can and regained operational control. *When is Captin gonna get here? I'm running out of time.*

Captin had an enviable reputation on the streets. He could get hold of anything and he remembered nothing, he was a trustworthy kinda guy. Maple had known him forever and guaranteed him, he could get me the necessary weapon and car to carry out my mission: go down to Quebec City, gather the intel, track down my mother, and blow up the lab to cover my tracks. The explosion part might be a little trickier, I didn't have the money to buy bombs off Captin, too expensive. And we didn't know any ISIS employees either. It was too bad, I'd have to improvise on the spot, labs are full of explosive materials, it's well-documented in every action film ever. With a bit of luck, I would find what I needed to blow the lab sky-high, along with half the capital at the same time.

We sipped cautiously at our cans. You can't be drunk when you're mid-negotiation. I could control my thirst, but Maple had a light arm. *Jesus, ease off a bit, it's not even noon hour.*

She scowled. *Well, you've certainly become full of yourself since you got rich!*

She was going to make me lose it again, she was already pressing up into her corner of the couch, in full sulk mode. I was just gearing up to play her game, reassure her and flatter her to re-establish contact, but then there was a knock at the door using our code: three little knocks, two big ones, and then three little knocks and another four little ones. Captin to the rescue!

Is it to kill Stony?

Maple seemed as surprised by Captin's question as I was. *No, why would you ask that?*

He lowered his voice a little, underlining the seriousness of his words. *I've heard people talking about the guy with the target on his forehead, it's not like there's a dozen of them around town. Seems like you got a beef with him, so I guessed you were gonna settle up and then get outta Dodge.*

I was flattered to be considered the potential killer of a notorious dealer. *I do owe him one, but—*

He lifted an index finger authoritatively. *Shhh, you don't need to explain yourself to me, you do what you gotta do. I just provide the tools. For the rest, the less I know, the better.*

Captin was a high-level criminal, but looked weirdly like a police officer. He wore a tight dark polo shirt over his muscular torso, he had virgin skin, a goatee, a good-boy haircut—even his waxed boots passed the test. He would have made an excellent pig, judging by appearances. But apparently you can't trust appearances. He unpacked the artillery from his backpack, three beautiful handguns. Connoisseurs will appreciate the value of the jewels on display: a Ruger GP100, 4¼-inch barrel with a shiny, wood-finished grip; a black matte Smith & Wesson M&P 22; and a chrome Sig Sauer P226 X5 X-Press. *Fantastic!* Even

Maple could see the quality of this arsenal.

I handled the toys one after the other, I hefted them, tested the resistance and comfort of the triggers. What a feeling of power! No, I should say what power, it was more than just a feeling. When you put a gun in a man's hand, he's already greater.

I wanna keep all three!

Captin chuckled, used to seeing his clients enthusiastic about such noble objects. *No problem, if you've got the money, but with the car waiting for you outside I think your budget's limited.*

He was right. I had to make do with just one.

I'll take the Sig Sauer! German weapons are reliable and have a long history of eliminating humans.

Captin agreed, recognizing that I'd made the right choice. *If you shoot point-blank, there won't be much of the head left, but I have to warn you, that gun is hot.*

I immediately agreed. *I know it's hot, that's why I'm taking it.*

Captin clarified his meaning. *No, I'm talking hot in the sense of risky. This piece has already been in a big shootout. If you get caught with it, they'll be pinning another charge on you.*

Poor Captin, if only he knew how many charges they'd already pinned on me, and all the ones to come. Even Atlas would have been weighed down by my charge sheet. *No stress, Captin, I want it, it's my baby.*

I slid the weapon into my belt immediately, enjoying the contact between the metal and my genitals. *Fuck yeah*, I was a fully paid-up gangsta, from the attitude down to the uniform. The cold, heavy steel stood between the world and me. Pressed up against my willing testicles, the powerful tool swelled my crotch. I guess on a symbolic level it was a pretty big deal too. I took two boxes of bullets, 9mm, classic and effective.

And finally, the car keys. A yellow Fiesta. I couldn't find anything better, but it should do the job. It was stolen at the airport last week, not reported yet. The owner will be back in three days, you have enough time to do your business and then burn the wheels. With the gun and the bullets, it comes to eighteen hundred, like we agreed.

Got my mind on my money and my money on my mind, I was humming happily. *What?* Captin obviously wasn't familiar with musical culture.

Oh nothing, it's just an expression where I'm from. Seventeen hundred, eighteen hundred! I counted out the money with extravagant gestures, the better to appreciate it before I handed it over to this arms dealer. *By the way, are you a Rimbaud fan?*

No. He never read poetry, just like everyone else. I took the keys, Captin told me where he'd parked the vehicle, automatic transmission guaranteed. *It's a done deal!*

Settling accounts makes good friends, but settlings of accounts make good enemies. Life had some accounts it owed me. I swore on my mother's head that Quebec City was going to take one in the face, right from the mouth of my gun!

9

REACTIVITY

Maple was a woman with a talented head on her shoulders and she was leading me to the gates of ecstasy. It was admirable—there was no other word for it, this woman had mastered some incredible techniques. She was generous too, this blow job was my third treat of the night. Not counting us fucking at the start of the evening. We didn't actually screw that much, she mostly decided it wasn't worth the bother of taking underwear off for the length of my performance. For an easy woman, she could certainly be difficult.

Despite her repeated favours, I still couldn't manage to fall asleep, damn insomnia. Maple advised me to crack open another beer, but I refused. As a responsible man, the director of operations, I wasn't going to wreck a key moment of my mission by getting drunk the night before.

There wasn't much of a mouthful left. Maple had come back to lie down by my side. *What are we gonna do with your mother, are we gonna bring her here?*

I hadn't got that far yet. To be honest, I'd barely dared to dream of the moment she would finally be in my arms. For me there was no need to plan for the after; that would take care of itself. My criminal life, full of traps, holes, heartbreaks, would get stitched back together and repair itself with my mother in it. That was the plan: find her and let destiny take its course. *We'll see.*

Sanchopanza was the first to react; it was his growling that alerted me. I yanked on my underwear and T-shirt, grabbed my gun, and woke up Maple. *Wake up, we need to get out of here.*

She groaned too and gave the mattress a tired thump. *What the fuck, I was asleep. Thought we said we were going to wait until rush hour. It looks a lot more suspicious at night!*

With my ears pricked, I ignored her complaints and tried to figure out what was bothering the dog. His growls were getting more insistent, I saw him on guard by the door. The cops were about to bust it down and the dog knew it. *Bodom bodom bodom.* I couldn't hear anything except my heart, which was about to explode, and its thudding in my temples. I didn't want to die, but I couldn't surrender.

Get up, Maple, we're leaving now!

Too late. *Badang! Crash! Crack!* The bedroom window smashed behind me just as the front door toppled down on Sanchopanza, whose little whimper of distress got lost in the racket.

Police! Get down on the ground! Bang!

A deafening noise accompanied the tear gas filling the room. I could barely make out the shadows coming into the apartment. Were there three, four, fifty? It was impossible to tell. First at the window and then in the direction of the living room I shot, shot, shot, shot, shot, shot, shot, shot, shot, and then shot a tenth bullet. When my cartridge clip was empty, I threw myself down on the floor, between the wall and the bed, to reload.

Get the Jesus fucking fuck out of here, you fucking cunty bastard Christ on a fucking whore bike douchebag fuckers! Maple was yelling at the top of her lungs, her voice cracked from the gas. She renewed my courage just when I needed it, and I got back on top.

We're evacuating, we're evacuating, two men hit, one hostage. Retreat, retreat!

A hostage? An excellent idea! *Move it, Maple, we're getting outta here!*

Coughing more than ever, she protested, but finally got up. *Arghghghg... I'm butt-naked, Jesus, I can't go out like this.*

Brandishing the gun amid the smoke, I grabbed her arm. Move it!

A second tear-gas bomb went off in the bedroom as we were leaving, and I fired two shots in the direction of the window. *Kpow! Kpow!*

My eardrums were ripped to shreds, and my eyes, which I was keeping open with a superhuman effort, were weeping hot tears, but we kept moving forward. Tiptoeing, I found the utensil drawer and grabbed a bread knife, one with good teeth. *I'm just going to hold this to your throat as we go out.* They wouldn't dare shoot an unarmed naked woman.

I don't want to fucking die, don't do anything crazy.

I had no idea what I was going to do, but I assured her I wouldn't do anything crazy. *Calm down, Maple, I know what I'm doing!*

The building's entranceway was smoky too, but less so. I could see in front of me, and as far as the floor. There was blood, a long trail of hemoglobin climbing back up the stairs to the exit. I followed it and found myself on the sidewalk, lit up by the flashing lights. Four cars were arranged in a semicircle around me. At the end of the block an ambulance was squealing around the corner.

Drop the gun, let go of the woman, you're surrounded!

Maple kept holding the blade and my hand to her throat. Should I flee behind the building or surprise them by rushing straight at them? Die confronting them or continue on my way? Pass them or pass away, so to speak?

Maple, I'm gonna save myself. We'll see each other again one day.

In a voice broken with love and devotion, she said yes. *Yes, we'll see each other again. I'll help; let go of the knife.* She slipped her hand under mine, grabbed the handle, and rushed forward, launching her naked body at all the officers who had us in their sights. Maple brandished the knife in front of her with one last yell: *Run, kiddo, run! Raaaaah!*

And I ran.

Bang bang! Bang!

Like a sponsored athlete, I ran. As I ran I fired in front of me, and behind me too. *Bang! Bang!* And I fired, and they fired, and I fired again, and they fired again. I felt a burning pain rip through my calf but I stayed standing, barely even slowing down. There would be time for suffering later; right now I had to prioritize. I fired even more, blindly. They responded, but I felt nothing. My time wasn't up, no, not yet...

Had Maple taken a bullet? It seemed likely. And that bullet wounded me too as it wounded my sweet friend. She had just revealed her true nature to me, she was a fallen angel, a human being in the most noble sense of the word, all animal, pure instinct and innocence. Imagining her injured or even killed twisted my heart, but it also spurred me on, it lengthened my stride, propelled me over fences even as I ripped the soles of my bare feet on the metal trellises.

They'd stopped shooting. But the lights and the sirens were close, too close. I had to keep running, run for Maple, run for my mother. I was widening the gap. Were they still following me or were they attending to the casualties? Had I injured enough of them to keep the whole cavalry busy? I prayed for that to be the case. And prayers have a habit of rewarding men with a can-do attitude.

I was in the street, the right street, the street with the car! There could be no doubt, I recognized it. Captin had assured us he'd left it there that very afternoon. But fuck, what side had he parked on? I couldn't guess, and there was not a second to lose. Bébette's face appeared in my mind: go left! I started running again, ignoring my feet, which were tearing more each time they hammered into the asphalt. I didn't give a shit, I had to find the Fiesta, and the Fiesta was found. A yellow car is as silly as a drunken auntie at a party but it's pretty damn easy to spot. *Holy Bébette, I thank you.*

Just as I was unlocking the door and diving headlong into the vehicle, Sanchopanza turned up on the sidewalk, breathless, with his twiggy little legs all wobbly. He'd survived the attack and followed me; he was just as loyal as Maple. Another sign from God: my mission was divine and Joan of Arc would have agreed. *Hop in, hound, you deserve your seat!*

The motor purred, and I was just heading out into the road when two police cars appeared at full pelt behind me, lights flashing. They immediately passed me. *Vrrrrm. Don't panic, just drive, get out of the area.*

I'd escaped, I'd escaped! Pretty much unscathed, just a bullet through my right calf, the soles of my feet totally massacred, and a ripped-off toenail. The car mat couldn't absorb any more of the blood my heels were bathing in. I needed to improvise a tourniquet before I lost consciousness, and fast. Sanchopanza's collar? Too short. I used my own belt, too bad if my shorts fell down. I managed to fashion a tourniquet, I would survive and so would my calf. But Jesus fuck, the pain was becoming unbearable. And Sanchopanza wouldn't stop licking up the blood from the bottom of the car. He might be loyal and have perfect timing, but man, that dog was disgusting, I had to shut him in the trunk.

Taking stock was the first order of business. Calming myself down to figure out what strategy to adopt became my priority. There were still a few hours of dark left, and I needed to stay on the island. Without a shadow of a doubt, the bridges were being closely watched. I would sneak out with an early-morning traffic jam.

In a dark corner of a badly lit parking garage, I could hide away in peace. Where should I start? *Shit, Maple...shitty shit shit, those dirty fucking shitty pigs!* I thumped the steering wheel with my fists. *Maaaaaple!* The tap started gushing again. Maple had sacrificed herself for me, she'd thrown herself at those armed men just to give me the chance to escape. I was overflowing with gratitude and shame. To think I'd considered dumping her, abandoning her, that very day! I'd come within a hair of doing it. Humans are like dogs: only the ones ready to die for us are worth having.

Sanchopanza's whining dragged me out of my sleep. The sun was at forty-five degrees, and the parking lot was half-full. It was almost ten. I couldn't believe I'd been asleep! As I yanked my gungy feet over the dried blood, I let rip with a virile moan. *Ggnnnnnnggghhh, fuuuuuck!* I was totally smashed up, I could barely move my right foot. But too bad, I was going to see this plan through. I'd made my decision, and it was as firm as a Viagra-fuelled cock. I had to forge on and not stop until I was in my mama's arms. After that, all would be well.

Sanchopanza must have been crying all night as well. Once he was released from the trunk, he slept on the passenger seat next to my gun. Around him and on the floor lay the vestiges of my punk period. I used the razor blade I'd confiscated from Maple to shave off my red mane, there was hair everywhere, even in the pins I used in my piercings. I'd managed to cover the tattoo decorating my forehead by pulling my boxers over my head, tucking the legs inside each other in a fancy updo. It wasn't actually bad-looking, I would even say it looked stylish, and there was a hint of Sikh turban about it if you looked at it from just the right angle. Fine, I was aware of the low probability of launching a fashion trend based on wearing underpants on your skull, but for the moment it was getting me out of a jam, giving me the bare minimum of anonymity on the road.

As I'd predicted, the traffic was heavy, slowed down by the thousands of construction zones, some of which were more abandoned and pointless than others. I wove in between two vans, I vegetated on the bridge for a long while, and then I got onto Autoroute 40. The June sun warmed the Fiesta, and a few clouds pursued me aimlessly. I was driving toward the capital, covered by legitimate rights and my 9mm. I was driving, but I was obeying the speed limits to the letter. It would be pretty fucking stupid to get nabbed by a pig with a radar gun now that I was so close to my goal. I was rolling along at 110, as cautious as an FLQ terrorist kidnapping a premier and a diplomat.

I was still a long way from Quebec City, but the radio was already spouting insane crap. It was incredible, in less then one hour this was the third station talking about me, or should I say lying about me. They were accusing me of having ambushed the police, pushing the hostage at them so I could get away, and some were even calling me a crazy gunman, a crazy angry gunman. *Jesus fucking Christ, I was defending myself! They were the ones shooting at* me!

I was shouting in the car, Sanchopanza was yelling too, we couldn't believe the media would let itself be manipulated like this. The only consolation was that Maple was alive, seriously injured but alive. Unlike the two police officers, two honourable upholders of the peace, model pigs and devoted fathers, who had died carrying out their duties trying to liberate the hostage and capture the dangerous Pinel escapee, blah blah blah.

For fuck's sake, I was asleep, I was sleeping peacefully with my whore, I wasn't any danger to anyone! Breathe, breathe, I needed to get hold of myself; my calf was starting to bleed again, and I was afraid I might faint with all these lies raising my hackles and my blood pressure. I'm a tolerant man, but spreading lies and warping reality isn't okay.

Changing the station was no use, I was on every channel. Even the ones that were pure advertising and insipid ballads interrupted their nostalgic pablum with special bulletins. They kept repeating that I was heavily armed and wounded. They'd be giving my description next, with worrying precision about my tattoos, including the target on my forehead. Lucky I was wearing my underwear on my head!

Being famous isn't all it's cracked up to be. With all those investigators dreaming of capturing me, my plan was compromised. And once I'd got my hands on the information about Mama, I had to make it back to Montreal, a return that would probably be less fawning than Martha Stewart's comeback reception. From the danger all along the route, when I arrived, and then on my way back, I'd have to bring my mother with me on the escape and hide out in the woods with her. And there was no guarantee that Maple and Bébette would agree to join us at our camp. Shit, things were looking bleak for my future. But as Borges, this blind guy who loved reading, would have said, *It's only in the darkness that the light shines. Have courage, Padawan!*

The traffic lights were stuck endlessly on red. I was hemmed in by an Econoline on one side and a van on the other. I should have stayed on the autoroute, but I was fucking famished. I regret it now. It was an error that undid everything, just ten minutes away from my goal, and all for a burger.

Actually I ordered four burgers, with fries and a large Pepsi. If you're going to take risks, you might as well make it worth doing. When I got to the window, the fat girl looked at me weirdly. Either she recognized me or my appearance impressed her, I couldn't say which. I grabbed the bag out of her hands, but I didn't have time to take my brown beverage. I think she must have spotted the gun on the passenger seat. Anyway, she took a step back and whined, *Help!*

I got back on the road at top speed, chain-swallowing the burgers. Three burgers and a large fries is pretty dry without a drink. Next to me, Sanchopanza munched on his burger hungrily. I hoped Mama wasn't allergic to animals, I was getting pretty attached to my doggie.

So now I was a cop killer, just like Ice-T. And not just once but twice! My teachers who used to tell me I'd never amount to anything must be kicking themselves now. I was the most wanted man in the country, maybe even in Canada! And that helicopter over the bridge was probably for me, and I could see flashing lights in my rear-view mirror as well. Shit, yes, it was for me! Before the traffic could move over to let the police car pass, I stepped on the gas and made myself a path, hitting the odd car to the left and the right as I passed. I took the first exit, widening the gap between me and the police cruiser, but the chopper was still right on me. I floored it, pushing the Fiesta to its limits, driving like a bullet down a street of hotels.

The cop car might have been less manoeuvrable, but it had a more powerful engine. It appeared in my rear-view mirror. Quick, I needed some strategic move to keep the cops busy and lose the chopper. I yanked the steering wheel and ran straight into the curb. A violent swerve lifted my car off the road. *Sqqqrrrk*, I was gliding! Paul Walker and his Porsche would have been proud of me. *Schhrrriiiick*, I retook control of the race car and landed in the parking lot of a big hotel. It was a big hotel that just happened to have glass doors at ground level. *Vrrrm-mmm!* Despite its burst tire, the car quickly picked up speed, enough to knock down a couple of tourists and smash its way in through the entrance, coming to a stop in the hotel lobby. It was an incredible entrance, but not exactly subtle.

People were screaming and running in all directions, except for the valet crushed under my car. I mean, he was screaming, yes, but he wasn't running anywhere. To make a long story short, I gathered up my dog, my gun, and my courage. I wanted to run, but electric shocks kept zapping through my body with every step. I limped on as fast as I could and reached the end of the hallway just as the police car crashed into my ride. I pushed open the exit door just in time. *Bingo!* A few metres to my right stood a rusty but spacious container. I gritted my teeth and staggered along the wall to my target, slid open the door, slipped inside the dumpster, and closed the door behind me. Allelujah, what a beautiful escape.

The reinforcements showed up en masse, ambulance sirens mixing with the city police and those of the Sûreté, just a hint sharper. The helicopter kept flying over my metal box at regular intervals for hours on end. Nobody could say they'd skimped on the efforts to try and track me down.

Luckily for me, this hotel had no ecological aspirations and refused to compost. I was swimming a metre deep in a sea of dirty sheets, cardboard boxes, and an unnameable stew, a mixture of all the week's unusable leftover food. If it hadn't been for this stinky, pulpy manna from heaven, the sniffer dogs would have tracked me down in no time.

By lying curled up in a ball under a blood-spattered sheet, which I admit is pretty gross, I avoided the inquisitive eyes of two smart police officers who came to peer in. One of them even stirred the trash with his stick, two inches from my face. *You were so close, douchebag!* I was a master strategist, so I'd had the presence of mind to break Sanchopanza's little neck as soon as I'd taken shelter in the dumpster, otherwise he might have attracted attention. Death in combat for his master, the most noble sacrifice of all. His corpse was bothering me, so I buried it in a corner, under a pile of chicken drumsticks.

The hours passed, night fell, but the pigs still stayed on guard, alert. They must have been searching every room in the hotel, and maybe even the hotels nearby. They reduced the duty officers in the early hours of the morning, but there were still three patrols and the same number of dog handlers occupying the parking lot opposite my hideout. I had no way of getting out, I'd be spending the day there. It was superhot inside the container. But I'm not one to complain, I had a hiding place and a fuck-ton of food. Room and board. Around noon, I dropped my guard, pulled the sheet up over my face, and dozed off, carried off by the sleep of the righteous.

10

ABNEGATION

It took four police officers to get me out of the container, after they'd smashed it open with a digger. The most muscly guy succeeded in getting my gun off me, breaking my fingers as he did so. My other hand was scrabbling at the bottom of my shelter, but I couldn't find my weapon. Working together, the long arms of the law lifted me out and threw me on the ground. I tried to get up, but my calf was shredded and useless.

There must have been twenty of them in front of me, but I was having trouble making them out, with their hazy silhouettes haloed by a blinding sun. The first one who came forward to beat me was Bébette. She kicked me in the jaw. *Didn't I tell you to be respectful to whores?*

Then the Sage came up and hammered on my skull with an illustrated version of La Fontaine's *Fables*. *You let me die, you moron!*

I was calling for help, but no sound would come out of my mouth. Denise's hand was crushing me and stuffing my mouth full of cereal, suffocating me with Cap'n Crunch. *There's nothing else you can say in your defence, you've been judged not criminally responsible.*

Edith came up and ground my balls with the heel of her thigh-high burgundy leather boots, musketeer-style, which didn't suit her at all. *Trust me, you're gonna pay for this!* In her arms, a naked, chubby baby—his body covered in tattoos all over except for his enormous erect penis—was holding his arms out to me.

I'll see you again one day, Papa.

And all around were dozens of animals: cats, warthogs, turtle doves, a polar bear, and Sanchopanza singing nursery rhymes.

I was woken up by a packet of still-warm egg rolls being dumped right on my head. I was about to protest when I suddenly remembered the dangerousness of my situation. Shit, I'd been asleep. For a long time. It was night again, this was the trash from dinner they'd just tossed in my face. I took a bite, it was tasty, and I stretched. My calf seemed to have scabbed over, although given the circumstances, there was a definite risk of infection.

I hate dreams, nightmares especially. But dreams are pretty revealing, they indicate a certain level of mental agitation. And I had to admit that the last few days had been pretty heavy on the plot twists and unforeseen developments. But what did that dream mean? It was a mystery. One day I would have to properly study dream symbolism, it's a fascinating science.

It had to be close to midnight now, the moon was stagnating at its zenith, the street was quiet. The time had come. Weapon in hand, I extricated myself from the dumpster. After one final goodbye to Sanchopanza, I limped across the parking lot as fast as I could. There were no police staking out the place, they must be looking for me somewhere else. But my wound and my tattered rags would likely attract attention. I had to procure myself some new threads and a new vehicle, asap. And without alerting the whole province, if at all possible.

Behind the endless row of hotels, there was an entire residential neighbourhood sleeping in the arms of exhaustion. Fatigue is the lot of all insignificant little wage earners. Crouched down, leaping from one yard to the next, I kept myself hidden while I looked for the ideal house, the most ordinary one, the least beautiful. I highly recommend stealing from poor people: they have fewer guns, fewer alarms, and fewer resources. In life just as in court, attacking poor people gives you a certain amount of immunity. This is well-known, recognized, and well-documented by court clerks.

I had my heart set on a modest bungalow that had given up all attempts at beautifying its grey bricks, a sign of poverty if ever there was one. There was one single car in the driveway, Japanese and anonymous. With a bit of luck, I was going to stumble upon a harmless old widow who was ready to offer me a three-piece suit and the keys to the vehicle. But I was still cautious, so I went around back of the hovel, just to introduce myself to it from behind. It's just a thing we do in our trade; breaking in through the front marks you as an amateur.

This was too easy. The bedroom window was open slightly. It's true the night was hot and AC is a luxury. I forced the frame, the mechanism gave way, and the window opened. Struggling to drag my injuries inside, I tripped and fell headlong onto the carpet.

I heard murmuring, a bedside lamp turned on, and a somewhat stifled cry rang out.

Silence. I don't want to hear a sound.

A young couple in their early twenties, kinda cute, were cuddled up at the top of the bed.

It's him, it's him!

I smiled, flattered at being recognized. *Yes, it's me, I see there's no need to introduce myself, so we're off to a good start.*

The woman started to moan and gripped her husband. *I don't want to die, please, we have a little boy, don't kill us.* The mother's blubbering woke up the proof of what she was telling me. In the next room could be heard an adorable little baby gurgle. *I'm a father too, I understand. You don't have anything to be afraid of.*

Not really reassured, the boyfriend begged me to put the gun down, he promised me he would collaborate fully even if I didn't have a weapon trained on his nose. I'm an independent worker, I don't take suggestions from anyone. *Shut your face, and start by getting up and giving me some clothes. No sudden movements or I'll shoot!*

Danny had a pretty nice wardrobe, considering his financial situation. And Annie had three different lacy outfits: one of them, a red one-piece with a hole at the crotch, seemed particularly sexy. Danny and Annie is pretty funny. Rhyming couple names! So cute.

He suggested a checked shirt, but I didn't like the pattern. He had some pretty fashionable hoodies, but it wasn't the season, Eventually I went with a Hard Rock Café Barcelona T-shirt. I've never been there, but it's still cool. For my lower half, I chose some old cargo pants with a baggy crotch, and to complete the look, a pair of running shoes two sizes too big. I'd just have to stuff the toes with newspaper when it was time to leave.

Is that today's paper?

He confirmed that it was and showed me the front page. *Mama's Boy in Quebec City!* And in big red letters too. Along with the old photo, and new ones from gas-station security cameras, and computer-generated pictures both with and without a target on the forehead. It reminded me that I could take my underwear off my head, I'd forgotten all about them. *Get me a cap, Danny!*

I was enthroned in the rank of immortals. As well as the front page, four other pages recounted my journey, with little tables giving key dates about my life, a list of my crimes, and other boxes explaining where the law had messed up, and another one to highlight Jamal's and Marcel's eyewitness accounts.

There's nothing like homemade shepherd's pie. It was much better than egg rolls and the other leftovers I'd been feeding on for the last two days. I tried to express my gratitude to Annie, but she wouldn't stop blubbering. Women always have to make a big deal out of things. Danny, more temperate, was rocking their little bundle of joy, barely three weeks old. *What's the kid's name?*

William-Alexis.

What a stupid illusion, an aristocratic first name won't be enough to drag him out of the muck. *Oh, okay. That's nice... I'll have some more shepherd's pie please, Annie.*

I was buttering my brown bread, which was actually pretty good, with my new fighting knife: a steak knife ready for battle. My gun was within reach, but I was feeling more and more confident about my little couple. We were good together. Annie was playing the part of the frightened shrew, but the tears weren't flowing any longer, it was just the soundtrack, tired crocodile tears. And she was giving me big helpings of shepherd's pie, so she couldn't hate me that much. After all, I'd only broken a window. And the baby had smiled at me in between two nursing sessions. Being part of a family was nice.

Behind all the closed windows and blinds, daylight was starting to break. I should have left now, but the human warmth kept me there. Annie had slathered my calf and feet in Polysporin to tend to my wounds. The antiseptic needed time to act, it was best to wait a few hours. *Do you have any cop shows we could watch?*

The second series fizzled out. Frankly, they exaggerated in Hollywood—no serial killer would let himself get caught by a lady investigator, however intuitive she was. But this new market reality meant producers had to reach their diversity quota just so they wouldn't have all the human rights groups on their backs. We were about to start the third season when Danny begged me to let him go to sleep, he couldn't handle anymore. I took a swig of his last beer before I checked the time. Almost midnight. We'd been bingeing on box sets, chips, and homemade comfort food since the morning. *It's been a great day!*

Annie turned the waterworks on as soon as I announced my night's plan, Operation Co-Sleeping. But they had nothing to be afraid of or to get their tear ducts in a twist about. To guarantee my safety and allow my body to scar in peace, I had to be sure of their docility. Despite the bonds of friendship we'd developed during our movie marathon, they might still call the police the second I shut my eyes. You never know, they might be tempted to betray me for the glory or a reward. Especially since they only had a single forty-inch television. I know it's not exactly dire poverty, but it's close. We'd have to sleep all together, joined at the wrists, with the baby snuggled up against me, for more sweetness and safety.

Annie slept badly. She was uncomfortable nursing the baby in bed, in front of an armed man who was spooning with her lover. He didn't sleep a wink either. I was amazed, the bed was super-comfy and I slept like a prince, barely bothered by William-Alexis's nighttime wake-ups. Once we were all detached, we held a family council in the kitchen. At my request, we had eggs and toast for breakfast, with soft fruit cut up just like in a restaurant. While the mistress of the house anointed my leg and feet with her healing balm, which was very effective, I outlined the part of my strategy that involved them.

I had hoped to please them by prioritizing their family values in my plan. I was expecting them to approve and encourage me to proceed. But that wasn't the reaction I got when I announced that I had to tie them up and gag them. I'll let you guess which one started bawling. Even Danny protested, worried that something unexpected would prevent me from contacting the authorities and setting them free, pleading that they had to take care of the little one. I immediately reassured them, nothing bad would happen, and I would tie up the baby with his face on his mother's breast. They followed my advice with resignation and swallowed a second breakfast. It would be a long day for them. I kept them company and ate another helping of scrambled eggs.

With pain in my heart, I left my new friends naked, gagged, and tied to their own dining table. I promised I'd get in touch once I'd got settled with Mama, we'd invite them to our house. With one final smile, I shut the door and locked it behind me.

Danny's car suited me as well as his clothes did. She drove like a charm. With the itinerary I'd printed out that morning, unknown to my hosts, I'd be at the forensic science lab in less than ten minutes, barring any complications, but God knows my life is certainly complicated. I was driving furtively, stopping at yellow lights, respectful of the dangerous cyclists and other foolhardy pedestrians. And I abstained from using the cellphone I'd borrowed from Annie. I was a model of excellent driving.

When I arrived at my destination, apprehension gave way to astonishment and then to disappointment. In my worst-case scenario, the heat had guessed my intentions and deployed a whole arsenal at the lab, ready to shoot on sight and do whatever it took to stop me from obtaining this vital information. In the best-case scenario, the lab would just be protected by a couple of its regular guards, two giants armed with automatic shotguns or machine guns, at a minimum. But all the synopses I'd imagined had one thing in common: I had a battle to fight, officers to kill, and a risk of dying a heroic death.

But no, the famous lab was all by itself, a simple concrete building, isolated, way out of town, just two storeys, barely even a sign to identify it. And it was right next to the autoroute too, which would make my getaway easier. No armed guards outside it. That's pretty crap, the government should take protecting our personal data more seriously, this is sensitive information we're talking about.

Nobody would have to lament gunfire today. I consoled myself with the thought that it was a sign, yet another one: I was on the right track, my goal had to stay focused on finding Mama rather than bigging up my own growing celebrity. I still believed that love could conquer death...

Demonstrating a remarkable sense of adaptability, I put my gun and my bellicose intentions aside. I found myself an isolated spot in the shade of a maple or some other conifer, and I set out to play the patience card. There were a dozen cars in the parking lot, which meant the same number of risks of alerting the police or seeing my plans foiled. Noon hour was approaching in leaps and bounds, all I had to do was wait until the end of the day and invade the building just before it closed. With a bit of luck, I could even leave Quebec City with all the information I needed without adding any corpses to my list of hits or any dead pigs to my growing collection. I just had to stay hidden in the shade, be patient, and remain calm.

You're gonna die, you sonofabitch! I'm gonna kill you with my own hands! I was getting emotional, I was better than that. But after a few hours on guard while listening to the local radio, I was contaminated. It's not healthy to bathe for too long in hate speech and advertising. By the end of the day, all I wanted was to yell at a loony leftie, get drunk at some bar, and gobble up a poutine at a shitty diner.

When the moron on the drive-time show came on air, my glass, which was brimming with anger, received one drop too many. It all started overflowing. I was prepared to recognize my own part in these wrongs, take responsibility for certain misdemeanours, maybe a little excessive violence, nobody's perfect. Even Princess Diana was an asshole. But to go from that to attacking me as if I was responsible for terrible atrocities, no way!

From his great height, the self-proclaimed free-thinking dropout talk-show host condescendingly listed my feats of arms. Then he launched into politics. He welcomed the motions from the opposition party, one calling for the Minister of Justice's resignation and one calling for systematic DNA sampling of everyone accused of violent crimes, regardless of whether or not they were convicted, not criminally responsible, or just had a shitty lawyer. Up until that point it was all fine, his ridiculous outbursts were entertaining me, but when he started demanding the death penalty for dangerous and unrepentant people with learning difficulties, it was one step too far.

I know, I know, we shouldn't feed the trolls, but nonetheless I felt the need to reply, I was going through a vulnerable period in my life. I regret it now, it was a bad idea, but it doesn't take anything away from my genius. The best of us can sometimes get carried away by emotion; Hemingway didn't just get good ideas running through his head, he had some epic fails too. And that day, my blood was as hot as his.

The researcher couldn't get over the fact that she had a celebrity at the other end of the line. *It is really you, you're not pranking me?*

I had to repeat my name half a dozen times. Fizzing over with excitement, she rushed to get me on-air with the presenter. Just from the tone of his voice I immediately understood that he was doing this to make his listener ratings shoot up, not to listen sympathetically to my legitimate irritation, my personal suffering, and all my extenuating circumstances. *I'm no psychiatric expert like those guys defending you in court, I'm just a citizen with an opinion, but with the number of murders you've committed I think society has a duty to protect itself. Between you and I, it's just common sense...*

It's grammatically incorrect to say between you and I, you should say between you and me. And I don't give a flying fuck about your citizen's opinion, if you were in my place you'd have done far worse. I'm not a monster, I'm a human being, and human beings can get better!

Radio silence. I avoided giving credit for the quotation so as not to inflate my prison psychiatrist's swollen head even more.

Well, for me and a good number of my listeners, we think that society would be better off seeing you dead rather than wreck itself trying to cure you!

That was when things got away from me, my words met up with my thoughts, and I explicitly threatened him with a slow death. I also swore I'd torture his listeners and remove their brains just to prove how porous their grey matter was. When I noticed my crimson face in the rear-view mirror, flecked with spittle, I realized I was starting to lose it. I promised to blow up the radio station and told him to have a nice day. *Have a nice day!*

This was a monumental error, the kind made by beginner

criminals and other amateur killers. I had taken a massive risk for nothing, this presenter was less of a threat than a kick from a person with no legs. I wasn't proud of myself—unlike that pussy on the radio, who kept going on and on about how he'd just interviewed the most wanted man in North America. He'd managed to pinpoint that I was in the area of Quebec City, and his station, always there for the well-being of taxpayers and ordinary folk, was going to collaborate with the forces of the law in the hope of facilitating my arrest. And my execution, which shouldn't be too long in coming… I turned off the radio.

Oh shit! On the floor of the car, I tried to destroy the cellphone with the knife. There's nothing worse than one of these devices for allowing the police to geolocalize you. I'd have to abandon the car too—once the cops had the phone number, they'd track Annie down and identify the vehicle I was using. Truly, that imbecile presenter had turned me into an imbecile too.

My plan was all turned on its head, I had to step up the pace and hope to get out of Quebec City before all the helicopters in the province started circling over the capital. I'd have preferred it if there was just one vehicle left in the parking lot, but the remaining three were less worrisome than the dozen there'd been that morning.

I was a rebel right down to the tiniest detail, so I started the car and went to park in one of the disabled spaces, right by the entrance door. It was a sensible move on my part, the security guy inside came out to meet me and bent down over the car. *Hello, sir, do you have a meeting?*

Pulling out my beautiful gun and my witty repartee in the same move, I replied, *Yes, I have a meeting with destiny!*

The receptionist was perplexed, watching the guard come back and wondering who the hot young man behind him was. From her desk, she unlocked the electronic door. *You okay, Pierrot?*

With a skilful nudge of the leg, I made the Pierrot in question stumble, the better to take aim at the secretary.

This is a holdup! That sounded a bit weird. *Well, not a holdup in that sense, but same idea. Put your hands up and get over here now!*

While the secretary was carrying out my instructions, I disarmed the guard. There was nothing to impress a regiment of cadets, his equipment was limited to a short baton and a decorative little cayenne-pepper shaker. I pocketed the lot as well as his cellphone. It might come in handy.

Since I didn't have any handcuffs, I tied up the junior staff with extension cords, sitting them back to back. I didn't skimp on the job, I trussed them up properly with four different cords. I needed to be able to work in peace. The whole time I was tying them up, the phone was ringing off the hook. I guess the receptionist didn't just sit around filing her nails when she wasn't getting tied up. Too bad she was old and chubby, otherwise tying her up would have been pretty exciting.

One of the white-coat dudes appeared at the bottom of the stairs. He was just as surprised as I was. I raced over to him and put my gun to his head. *What's up, doc?*

He dropped both his calm manner and his files on the floor. *Nothing, nothing's up.*

That jerk actually answered me! *I don't give a fuck about your life, douchebag, I want all the information you have on Marie-Madeleine Fontaine, it's urgent!*

In some kind of technical jargon mixed with stammering and snivelling, he managed to explain to me that all the files were electronic, he would need to go back to his workstation upstairs.

He docilely replied to all my questions: yes, he was alone here with my two prisoners; no, he wouldn't try any funny business; yes, the file should have my mother's address in it.

Alright, off we go!

Before we went upstairs, I warned the two juniors that I would kill the good doctor if they tried to get free or call for help.

At long last, I had Mama's address in my hands. My family nest was at 1339 Rue Ontario Est, apartment 3, in Montreal. Rue Ontario! What a plot twist, I must have passed by that building dozens of times, but I'd had to risk my life, kill people, refine a thousand tactics, and journey to Quebec City just to come back to Rue Ontario and finish my quest. It was like I was in an adventure novel with added sugar-coated spirituality, just about to learn a great life lesson full of meaning and hope. *Let me live...*

You shut your face, I'll decide that! I couldn't get over it, there wasn't a single explosive, combustible, or fire starter to be had anywhere in the whole building. Shit, I really wanted to get back to town, but I had to blow this place sky-high and burn my tracks. My three pinkos would raise the alarm as soon as I'd got outside. I wasn't managing to think with my usual sharpness. How could I buy enough time to get back to Montreal before they discovered I'd been here, before they realized I'd found the information I needed and intended to put my family back together?

I thought about assassinating the three of them, but they didn't have weapons, and it wouldn't do my reputation any good. Maybe they had children or families, I couldn't allow myself to leave too many orphans in my wake, that's just my own personal sensitivity. There was no choice, they'd have to come with me in my escape. *Alright, doc, move your ass. We're going back down!*

There was a surprise waiting for us when we got back down. I held my gun to his cheek, ready to blow his head off with a 9mm bullet. *And who's this fucker?* The jerk had been untying my hostages! Mr. Moustache lay down on the ground of his own accord. *No, no, please don't shoot!*

The receptionist answered me. *He's the janitor. He comes every night after we close, he couldn't have known…*

I shot and shot and shot again. I knew that after a few hours someone would report the disappearance of these employees. The cops would show up and see that some files had been consulted, so I fired at the main server of their computer system. That might give me another couple of hours. And it would really piss off the civil servants.

The doc had a magnificent truck, this year's model, perfect for group road trips. I bundled my hostages in before I discovered the supreme annoyance: manual transmission! Oh well, following in the tradition of all successful pimps and other chamber of commerce notables, I would have a driver. I sat down in the back seat, next to Monique the receptionist, the most unstable, the biggest nagger, and the most likely to cause problems. But with my gun in her side, she knew to keep hold of herself.

Don't pull no stupid shit and we won't have no stupid corpses. We're all going to Montreal together, and I'll set you free when the time and the place are right.

It was going to be a long journey, I started up a guessing game, but they were terrible, even the doctor. Just one more proof that high-level studies can be bought, and they aren't worth shit.

My generosity had saved me. The autoroute rolled out ahead of us like a red carpet, while alongside us, the single men occupying the other lanes were getting their vehicles stopped and searched by the pigs. I'd never seen so many. There were more pigs on Autoroute 40 than in a bacon factory. We even passed a roadblock just by Repentigny. It was a monster traffic jam, more than three hours of waiting. With my gun pressed into the secretary's ribs and our triptik in my head, our driver would never have dared to reveal my identity. But I was pretty scared, I admit.

The cop leaned over and cast an eye around the vehicle, didn't ask me to take my cap off. He asked the doc where we were headed.

A conference about criminal identification, officer sir! He spoke a little too clearly for my taste, but the officer in question, clearly annoyed at having to direct traffic, ordered him to carry on. *Off you go, doc!*

Straight ahead, the Montreal towers rose up, like enormous dicks marking the harbour entrance where I would bring my *Titanic* into port, safe and sound. Except for Sanchopanza, who was condemned to stay in Quebec City forever. It had been a necessary sacrifice. On the outskirts of the city, I breathed its stale air deep into my lungs, I filled myself with its aromas at the riverside, scents of vice and refineries, happy to be back. In the right place and the right time, I was about to achieve my mission. I was going back home.

11

STEALTH

Stony was stunned to see my face, especially given that my face showed up along with a delegation of four hostages freshly kidnapped from the capital.

Hey, Stony, I have money for you!

Before the idea of smashing his skull into my teeth could occur to him, I held out a big wad of green bills, five hundred bucks in small denominations. He signalled to us to go in. Money talks and men listen.

You can do anything with money, including wipe your ass or start a fire. For me, it was now just a way of achieving my goals as quickly as possible. In Montreal, you can get whatever you want if you speak the right language and have a fistful of dollars. Even if you're part of the francophone minority, you can make yourself understood with enough ready cash. So we'd stopped at an ATM to withdraw the maximum possible from each one of my road-trip companions' accounts. It was a nice little jackpot, nearly three thousand dollars. The janitor was spared, he only had thirteen dollars left in his savings account, poor guy! Anyway, you can't take out anything less than twenty.

With the end of my gun, I made my hostages sit down on

the floor, on the old grey living room carpet, next to three dozing crackheads. I put the money in Stony's hands.

I'm sorry, man, I didn't know you were...

Surprise, surprise: now the dealer wanted to repent. That's the power of popularity and money—with a little of each, even your former sworn enemies are all gung-ho about eating out your asshole.

The important thing is that you do what I say. Win-win, you keep the cash and I gain some time!

His smile was less trustworthy than a car dealer's tax return, but I needed his collaboration, and for the moment that was all that mattered. *I need an hour, just an hour. You keep an eye on my hostages and let them go afterward, okay?*

Saying nothing is the same as consenting, so Stony agreed.

I crouched down in front of my prisoners, who'd become my friends over the time and all the stress we'd been through together, it's a kind of syndrome that was popular in Stockholm, Europe. *See, I don't wanna kill you. Listen to Stony, he's a good guy, and don't try to leave ahead of time or he'll kill you. Deal?*

I hugged them all and kissed Monique, with the promise that everything was going to be fine, which didn't stop her trembling. She was a vulnerable leaf at the mercy of the wind of panic. I felt very tender toward her. If she hadn't been so ugly, I might have found her cute.

Stony promised me he'd give Bébette a kiss from me and give her my poem. It was a ten-verse haiku in which I invited her to start a sexual revolution with me, without placards. It was romantic, funny, and erotic, and I thought she'd probably get it framed in memory of us. And when I came back for her in her turn, I would whisper it in her ear and she would fall more in love with every line, and then we'd have great sex and then she'd get up and cook me a steak while she wore a garter.

Enough with the fantasy. I snorted a long line of cocaine on the edge of the counter and swallowed down two tabs of speed to maintain my mental sharpness and the adrenaline I'd need for the final part of the operation, which I'd called Operation Final Part.

That was good stuff, thanks, Stony. I don't have any time to waste. I'm off to confront my destiny.

He allowed me to give him a manly hug. I raced down the stairs and ran toward Rue Ontario.

I could feel the noose tightening. When I'd returned to the island, the radio was already announcing the liberation of two hostages and a baby as well as reporting the disappearance of four employees from the forensic lab.

This murderer on the lam, nicknamed Mama's Boy and the Beast, is the prime suspect.

Smart fucker! But I figured I would still be able to rebuild my family before I got shot at by the police or poisoned by the secret service. Everything was still possible, even happiness.

The cops had no way of knowing whether I was back in Montreal or still in Quebec. But even so, the streets of Montreal were already crawling with police cars, police on bikes, police on foot. I had to use every ounce of my ninja artistry, my knowledge of stealth movement, and other commando techniques. The fact that I was very familiar with the neighbourhood worked in my favour; I could go through parking lots, yards, and alleys.

I should have gone straight to Mama's house, but I'm a principled man, there's nothing I can do about it. What's the point of reaching destiny if you don't do it in style? For the sake of friendship, I had to help Maple the way she'd helped me. There was a whore on her block, but Maple wasn't there. That hysterical prima donna Cookie was in her spot. She'd been totally out of touch with reality since her brain injury: a car had struck her as she was leaving a Vietnamese bar where Bryan Adams had fucked her at the end of the last millennium. She told this story constantly, it was her moment of glory.

Pssst, Cookie, over here, come here!

She tottered over to join me in the shade of a building that was being renovated. *Jesus Christ, look who's back in town!* She was going to get us noticed, the silly cow.

Ssshhh, Cookie, don't be stupid!

We slipped underneath the scaffolding to talk more easily. *You have any cash, babe? I've never jerked off a cop killer before, it turns me on!*

It didn't turn her on at all, I knew her shtick. But her powder habit forced her to offer herself to all and sundry. This was a woman fascinated by the scents of cocaine. To be able to appreciate its aromas, she sniffed several grams of it every day. Cocaine was an expensive curiosity.

I do have some cash for you, Cookie, you'll be able to powder yourself all over, but you have to help me first. Where's Maple?

Beautiful Maple, she's inside, babe. For a long time. She was already on probation, they accused her of armed assault on a police officer. They don't forgive that. And now she's in deep shit all because of you, babe!

Torn between the desire to shove my fist into Cookie's traumatized skull and the desire to feel sorrow over my friend's fate, I kept my calm. *She's the one who decided to attack them, we're all responsible for our choices, you should read Malraux sometime.*

The old whore didn't give a shit about great literature and asked me what I wanted, why I was preventing her from working. *Whaddya want, babe?*

I fanned out the bills and her face lit up, then I pulled out my gun and that shifted things.

There's sixteen hundred bucks there. In the reflection of her eyes I could see her building a cocaine Kilimanjaro.

Wow, babe, you're making big bucks.

I was making a mistake, there was no doubt about it, but when you're loyal like me, you have to stay coherent. *It's money for Maple. To help her pay her lawyer. Tell her to use mine. He's good.*

Cookie pouted, disappointed to find out that the money wasn't for her. It was a fake pout, I could hear the cogs working in her crafty mind, she was already planning to rob me.

Listen, Cookie, I'm gonna add two hundred bucks for you. And if you really give the money to Maple or the lawyer, I'll get you another five hundred a week from now. Okay?

Oh. Okay, babe! All smiles, she grabbed the wad out of my hands.

I immediately pressed the gun under her chin. *But if you mess up, Cookie, I'm gonna come back and blow your face up once and for all.*

Nobody likes being threatened. She slapped me with the back of her ring-laden hand.

You don't just have bugs in your underwear, your head's full of them too! She slipped the money into her bag before saying her farewells. *I'm gonna do it for Maple, not for you, I've always hated you!* Cookie was overreacting, faithful to her reputation.

Why'd you call me babe then?

Cause you're full of shit!

I didn't take it personally; she was a few sandwiches short of a picnic. I'd done what I'd had to do, and if Cookie didn't die of an overdose during the night, Maple would get her money along with a wink from a true friend. But no media would be there to document it.

There could be no doubt it was my mother's building; they'd known I'd show up there sooner or later. There were two police cars out front, one behind, and another two quietly minding their own business on either side. Even though I'm better than Miles Davis at improvising, I was wondering how on earth I could breach the defences. Especially as the clock was ticking. Once they got confirmation I was back in town, they'd be sending even more reinforcements.

A summary scout around made me notice how close the neighbouring triplex was. From the roof, I could work out which one was Mama's apartment and choose the best approach. Crouching down, I slipped behind the tired brick building. Clinging to the frames and railings of the balconies, I hoisted myself up with all my strength, ignoring the shooting pains in my murdered calf. I made it to the top of the triplex and found myself on the roof. It was an ideal observation point.

So ideal, in fact, that it looked right over Mama's place. I crawled to the back of the building, which adjoined the back of the triplex I wanted so much, practically sitting ass to ass with it. And on the third floor of said triplex, a young pig was standing guard outside my mother's glass door, busy texting love letters to his mistress, or his gay lover, or a godfather from the Estonian mafia for whom he carried out occasional contracts. Who knows.

They hadn't evacuated my mother or cloistered her far away from me as I had feared. They'd just secured her in place. My mother, attached to her routine, must have refused to be expatriated from her apartment. Or maybe it was another equally noble principle: she systemically refused to do what the pigs said. In either case, I was proud of her.

My emotions were all muddled. When I saw a shadow pass by the window, my heart wrapped itself up like a Christmas present. It palpitated even harder when the frosted bathroom window lit up; Mama was in the bathroom! She was just there, right in front of me, twenty metres and a few feet away, Mama was doing her business!

Three floors down, two plain-clothed police officers were talking on the sidewalk. Those plus the one stationed at the door to the family home meant I had three cops to neutralize, and I didn't even have a silencer. Luckily, the amphetamines were stimulating my synapses, all the possible options ran through my head, and I stopped at the right one. *When the path to destiny seems blocked, you have to just barge straight through*, according to Gandhi, an Indian lawyer who specializes in online quotations.

Getting down was even more dangerous than going up. The railings threatened to give way, I was at risk of plunging to the ground and drawing attention to myself, or dying before my time. Once I'd arrived on the ground, I limped at top speed, headed two blocks over, where the security perimeter was more lax, and I waited for one long minute, then two.

A supercute teen couple appeared, a white guy and a black girl. The dude wasn't bad-looking, but she could have done way better. All the kids have phones glued to them these days, and a phone was what I needed. As soon as they were level with the bus shelter where I was spying on them, I stuck my knife in the boy's shoulder. Barely—I must have thrust it in two inches max, but it stayed stuck in his flesh. It was stubborn. The guy was moaning, but not loud enough. And the girl was frozen, no use whatsoever.

Quick, call the police! I encouraged her.

She started screaming eventually. And she inspired her man, so he started doing it too. Some upstanding citizens would stop and call for help, I mean, we're part of a civilized society after all, right? With their cries of terror in the background, I trotted along faster and hid behind a car that was parked alongside the building I'd just climbed. Just in time. It must have been buzzing through on all the radio frequencies in the area. The two pigs on the sidewalk yelled an order to their colleague stationed up with Mama before they jumped in their car and went to find the action, two streets over.

I immediately crossed the road. With all the noise of the sirens and the excitement kicking off in the neighbourhood, the Sûreté's finest didn't hear me coming up the stairs. When he lifted his eyes from his phone, it was to see the barrel of my gun pushed up to his nose.

No sudden movements, asshole, I'm not afraid to use it. And he was well-placed to know.

I took his gun, less powerful than my own, and cuffed his hands behind his back. This valiant agent of the law was trembling more than a vibrator, but he still tried to threaten me. *You're making a big mistake, you won't get away this time!*

I pressed my gun to his windpipe. *Maybe I won't get away, but I can certainly make sure you go away. So shut your douchehole.* I made him turn around to face Mama's door and I knocked.

Behind this door I was going to meet death, and my mother. In that disorder.

My mother first, who opened the door to the police officer. I pushed him inside, made him lie down on the floor, and locked the door closed behind us. After all this effort and all these corpses and tears, I was finally there. I was at Mama's house, with Mama, with my family. I'd succeeded. I'd never doubted that I would, but I couldn't believe it.

I lifted my eyes the way you might hoist a ton of bricks with broken arms. I couldn't breathe anymore, my chest was crushing everything I had in the way of a heart, but in spite of everything I kept looking up. Her bare feet on the worn linoleum, her faded dark blue dress, her bare, skinny shoulders, over which her hair cascaded, red and grey.

I had to come up to her face, show her mine, look in this woman's eyes, this mother I'd missed so much, for so long. I was afraid I might faint, or sweat out my last remaining strength, but I mobilized everything I had left with a superhuman effort and lined my eyes up with hers.

It was her, really and truly her, beautiful and old. I would have sworn on her head: it was my mother! We hadn't seen each other for more than twenty years, but the proof was sending long shivers running up and down my spine.

Pretty much down to the wrinkle, it was the exact same Mama they'd ripped me away from two decades earlier, as if it was yesterday. A tear spilled out and snaked down my cheek.

And I was recognized at last. *You've found me again, David.*

12

OPPORTUNISM

lthough dreams are sometimes too beautiful to be true, reality is never too ugly to be false. I threw myself into Mama's arms, but she closed hers before I could do it. She didn't let me take her in my arms. Didn't let herself be embraced. She let me split in two, break, crumble in front of her. I was trying to find her gaze but could only find her eyes. Nothing for me. She ripped the smile off my face. *But, Mama...*

I'm not your mother, I'm nobody's mother. I did my best, but it couldn't have been worse. Look what you've become, a soul wandering in the shadows, a sinner. Dear God, I don't want to hear any more about you, you're my cross to bear, my cross that's too heavy to bear.

I noticed half a dozen crucifixes in the living room and an annotated Bible on the table, which explained all this Christian babbling.

But I love you, Mama!

She clenched her fists and spat out my death warrant. *How do you think I could love you? You're a murderer, a rapist, a sinner of the worst kind. God has abandoned you!*

It was like a bomb in my heart, my head, my calf—a rusty lance thrust into my wounds. I staggered, I fell, I put one knee on the ground. *You are too, Mama. You're abandoning me too.*

Mama didn't even hold a hand out to me, she left me on the carpet and started reciting "Our Father." I struggled to drag myself up, stunned. Our pet policeman tried to do the same, but hobbled by the handcuffs, he collapsed on the tiled floor. Despite the humiliation of his fall, he chuckled nastily, looking at me and shaking his head. *I warned you, you pathetic jerk.*

BANG!

The impact of the bullet ripped off half his head, sending it scattering in all directions, three metres away from his body. Mama and I got chunks in our faces and eyes.

I had ordered him to shut his mouth, I'd warned him. The police have to obey orders just like everyone else. Now he has to take some responsibility.

Mama jumped, but she didn't change her tune. *Murderer! Go on, kill me too, violence is all you know, and evil, you're evil incarnate!*

I raised my weapon, and even though it was stronger than I was, I didn't shoot. Behind the veil of tears and blood fogging up my vision, I saw her silhouette moving. She was brandishing her fists at me and hurling insults. *Pharisee, sodomite, I hate you!*

In the winter of our disreunion, the van of reality had smashed into the doe of my illusions. My mother's coldness was all too familiar to me. Fragments of memories were coming and ripping my heart open with the violence of the slaps she'd given me, with the hand that never caressed me, never made me any meals, never brushed my hair, never touched me, never rested on my forehead when I was sick, never consoled me, never wiped away tears from my damp cheeks. Suddenly, the truth leapt up and hit me in the face, no denial or lies possible. Mama had never loved me, and in this case, past performance would definitely be a guarantee of future performance.

The point of no return is not the point of impact. It's the moment when you realize that your momentum is too great to stop yourself from crashing into the wall you're barrelling toward. The point of no return is the choice between slowing down and stupidly injuring yourself, or crashing and shattering into a thousand pieces. Like a missile, a suicide bomber, or Ayrton Senna. Irremediably.

I don't know you, my son. I'm with Jesus now. And she turned her back on me.

Blood was trickling into my eyes and mouth, tufts of hair were stuck to the gun's sight, but I wasn't crying anymore. I was hitting her over and over, holding the gun to her forehead, but I couldn't shoot, so I hit her, took aim again, pressed the gun into her throat, but couldn't find the resolve to shoot, hit her even more—because she wasn't stopping me, wasn't patting my back like Bébette, wasn't understanding me like the Sage, wasn't stroking my neck like Maple, wasn't trusting me like Edith, wasn't consoling me like Denise, she was doing nothing, nothing except sighing more and more quietly.

The hand of God grabbed my gun. Maybe I was also exhausted, or just so I couldn't fight anymore, or carry on hitting my mother. I stopped. Bubbles of blood blew in and out of her nostrils. She was still alive, but I wasn't. It was enough. I didn't want to kill anybody anymore, I preferred to offer myself up.

Mama was gasping. She managed to open one of her unbearable eyes, and wailed, *Why, my son?*

I hurt too much, my internal void was filling up with tears and blood, I was drowning. I was dying too much to carry on living. I left her on her kitchen floor. I was going to kill myself. And that was all she'd taught me, to suicide your way out of your problems.

Drunk with distress, I staggered to the bathroom. Leaving Mama to her dying moments and her crucifixes, I shut myself up in the tiny room and, at long last, exploded. *Noooooooooooo! No, no, noooooooooo!*

The yell wasn't the least bit therapeutic, contrary to what old Doc Mailloux always used to claim. I was suddenly buried under the burden of shame I'd been dragging around for my thousand bad choices. A violent fatigue stabbed at my soul, the idea floating in my skull grew, became a throbbing pain, increasing, taking up all the space, seeming urgent. I needed to die.

I was trembling, shivering, wailing, and struggling to rummage through the bathroom. *Mamaaaaa, why did you do this to usssss?*

We always end up hanging ourselves with our own heartstrings. I found and gulped down all the available tablets, throwing them down my throat in handfuls. I chewed up and swallowed her entire drugstore.

Sitting on the edge of the bath, I took my gun, and the cop's gun, and placed one on each temple. It was time to go. The meds were already blurring my senses, numbing my body. I could hear my mother's gasping, the bubbles of blood she produced with each breath. My own bubble had burst. All that was left was to blow off my head.

BANG! BANG! I pulled the triggers, but my heart wasn't in it any longer. The huge din of windows and doors being kicked down, deafening grenades, and the industrial quantities of gas, I knew that the tactical squad had turned up. They were using the cavalry to hunt down Mama's Boy. Just to respect my own reputation, I answered back with a few bullets.

BANG! I fired one last shot toward the door in legitimate defence. *Fuck the police!*

They had to one-up me, and I took another bullet in the calf! Same leg too, you couldn't make it up. Mama's medication was carrying me far away from human misery, far from the turpitude of mortals. My hands were cold, paralyzed. My wonderful German ally fell to the floor, and the disfigured pig's gun too. Defeated, I slipped down onto the tiles. On my knees before destiny, I took a second bullet in the clavicle. *Bang!* I was anaesthetized, so I couldn't feel anything anymore, but it was still an unbearable pain. I screamed the first word in the world one last time before I collapsed: *Mamaaaaaa!*

A white light guided me toward the darkness. I was finally going to make it, reach the warrior's rest, the eternal sleep of the righteous. The tactical squad crashed through the bathroom door at the very same moment the Grim Reaper picked me up under the armpits. I was escaping them one more time, death had taken me before they could.

13

FAME

Death is a state of mind; once the mind has returned to the state of a free soul, the shadows soften and then light up suddenly. Reassured, I understood that I was part of an everything, that a part of everything that existed inhabited me, and vice versa. No judgment possible. Sorry to disappoint the paid-up evangelists and other fundamentalists, death is merciful. No big deal, nothing serious, human existence is a cosmic sigh, a pleasant insignificance. From the other side, even thought blanches, just like a cheese string. Sometimes a little unconsciousness is soothing.

The movie of my life played behind my closed eyelids. It was pretty emotional seeing myself as a child, playing with nobody. All the apartments, the foster homes, and the prisons I'd dragged my anxiety around scrolled past, all the schools where I'd failed and failed, stretched across the canvas of my biography. And the animals I'd loved, the women I'd caressed, the drugs that had consoled me, the weapons that had built me, all the details of my existence played in a loop like the trailer for a promising feature film. And I was rapping the soundtrack myself, accompanied by hot ladies wearing sequinned dresses and humming harmonies behind me. A big beat for a big destiny. It was pure joy.

An angel took me by the hand and walked me across the screen. Blinded, I could no longer make anything out, but I felt somehow pulled, and then I was breathed into a narrow, transcendent tunnel, like some kind of spiritual vagina. I was going to meet my creator, come face to face with the animal named God. I was ready, serene, at peace.

I saw the light. But it turned out to be a nurse's flashlight. He was swinging the luminous beam from one eye to the other as he took my pulse with his free hand. *Your condition is stable, the doctor will come and see you soon.*

I'm alive?

The nurse, who was clearly feeling confused about his sexual identity in my presence, gave a nervous puff of laughter. *Well yeah, the clavicle's not exactly a vital organ, nor the calf...*

I'd failed at suicide, or life had succeeded, whichever way you want to look at it. Even the tactical squad hadn't managed to kill me. It spoke volumes about how tough my hide was. What a miserable miracle, here I was in hospital, handcuffed and strapped to a stretcher. Back to square one, a clavicle, a calf, and a few illusions down.

Three policemen were in my bedroom, and two more were keeping watch outside the door. Luckily, the rights of man were on my side, otherwise they might have been tempted to take revenge. Like every other armed gang on the planet, the police stand in solidarity with their corpses. Vendetta is a noble instinct, but in a hospital, with witnesses, and where criminals' rights are respected, these five pigs had their hands tied as tightly as I did.

I like to practise humility, but you have to admit it's pretty validating. Following the example of grandmasters of the past, we recognize the value of a criminal by the number of low-ranking personnel he can mobilize. But my restraints did remove all possibility of escape. Given my condition, it was better to rest, regain my strength, and eat delicious fruit compotes served in individual portions. Not that I'd have shared them anyway.

The doctor confirmed that it's impossible to die from swallowing twenty aspirin, some St. John's Wort, and a bunch of laxatives, and he was pretty skeptical that I'd even really lost consciousness. Jerk. Death is a personal experience, it's like love, but less permanent.

I was dead, you douche! You don't know anything!

Nobody would ever have admitted it, but the entire hospital staff wanted to see me. Even the gynecologist had to find an excuse. It was constant traffic in my room. I guess it was a mixture of admiration and morbid curiosity. Everyone wanted to see the Beast, naturally.

Like all geniuses, criminal or otherwise, I polarized opinion. I could see just as many fascinated faces filing past as horrified ones. That's always the way, whatever is better than us teaches us or crushes us.

After a few seconds of scrutinizing me, they practically all came to a contemptible, if not downright mistaken, thought. Things like: *I thought he would be a bit burlier... He doesn't really look that bad... Is it him that smells so weird?* But their disappointed expressions didn't bother me. Monstrosity is like beauty: it's what's on the inside that counts. Injured, locked up, handcuffed to a hospital bed, I was less impressive than if I were standing tall, proud, and armed, obviously, but if they just untied me for two minutes I'd shove their mocking smiles right down their moronic obedient asshole civil servant throats.

I'm calm, more zen than a llama. I figure smashing in Mama's head was a kind of catharsis, setting off some therapeutic mechanism. I would have tried anything. The ball is in her court rather than in my head. At least she knows that I love her and I'm ready to reunite. I was keen to get news of her. The newspaper told me she was recovering in a nearby hospital. For reasons that escape me, they've forbidden me to make contact with her, even over the phone. Too bad for me, and especially for her, I wanted to apologize and I'd written her an acrostic poem using her name.

But it's just a delay. I'll have other opportunities to contact her, using lawyers as go-betweens if necessary. Despite the intensity of our most recent family drama, nobody died. Except for a policeman, but that was in the line of duty and they get paid for that, so it doesn't count.

I don't want to minimize my own actions either. I nearly killed Mama, and I died a little bit myself. We were right at the threshold of tragedy.

So I guess I didn't end up dying at the end of this book. I didn't kill myself. There's no shame in it. Suicide is a very personal thing, it's nobody else's business. I'll kill whoever I want to, including myself, without having to pay for it. I am a free man.

In another week or two, once my clavicle's had a chance to knit together and my twice-afflicted calf is more solid, they're going to send me back to Pinel while they wait to see if there's any way they can try me in court. Was I criminally responsible this time? My lawyer still thinks I'm the most irresponsible person in the entire world, which bodes well. He can't get over all the work I'm bringing his way. Even with the pittance paid by legal aid, he must have a whole garage full of sports cars.

Whichever it is, prison or Pinel, I have to get used to the idea that I will never be free, and always excessively monitored. It's all a question of dangerousness and the credibility of the system. I've killed a few too many people, my face has appeared in the newspapers, and half an entire department has had to resign in the fallout.

Always eager to bring out a culinary reference, my lawyer confirmed that I would forever after be a "hot potato." I was distractedly listening to his spiel with one ear, savouring my fifth compote of the day.

Any normal citizen, inoffensive and insignificant, would have panicked on seeing all his possibilities for freedom collapse around him, but I'm a philosopher in my soul, so I just laugh. I no longer had anything left to do outside anyway. I'd done a ton of drugs, built myself a solid reputation, benefited from Maple's friendship and Bébette's love. Above all, I'd found my mother, even if our reunion was less joyful than I'd expected. My son will certainly be able to be proud of his father, a great example of determination, a famous and celebrated man. Deep down I will love them all even more, and vice versa. People are always easier to love when they're not there.

With my incredible brain, I'll find something to keep me busy behind those walls. I'm thinking of writing novels, people tell me I have a way with words. I could also sell paintings, like Charles Manson. He was less prolific than me, but he's popular too. But ultimately, with my street experience and the three little pigs I've huffed and puffed to death, I think my future really lies in gangsta rap. I just need to convince Dr. Dre or Jay-Z to invest in me and build a professional studio at Pinel. Why not? After all, plenty of homeless organizations have choirs, so why not psych units?

Over the shoulder of the vengeful policeman who was

refusing to massage my oh-so-painful feet, the sky was darkening. Through my grilled window, Montreal stood out against the dusk. The city was going to sleep peacefully tonight. I imagined the credits of my adventure scrolling up, superimposed on the setting sun. But don't forget: I'm likely to slip a few powerful twists into the epilogue.

EPILOGUE

Only *God can judge me*, and even at the last judgment he won't judge me! God is love and forgiveness, which is handy. My experience as a man returned from the dead has plowed my fallow spirituality. I've decided to believe in Jesus, the saints, the archangels, and all their various permutations. It's a considered and highly strategic choice; maybe it will turn into a kind of faith along the journey. Fake it till you make it and all that. Eating sparks an appetite, and that's true for those holy-wafer snacks as well.

The liturgical chanting creates a nice ambience at Pinel. We're just a bunch of devout people accompanied by some lay psychopaths chanting our gospel every Sunday morning. A prayer corner has been provided for us Christians at great expense, just next to the Muslim nook. Our choir was way better than their atheist duet. Simon is no longer the only one to have chosen God and his secondary characters. Pinel is being converted before your very eyes.

After nine months of reflection, Mama decide to renew our bond. In the end, all it took to make her see reason was a few punches in the face and some poems with a Christian flavour. Women always need to feel wanted, and mothers are women just like any other. Even being ravaged by pregnancy and single parenthood doesn't make them any less flirtatious.

My crusade has helped me reach my mother through Christianity. So much the better, since that was the main reason I converted. Now we have to steep all our family conversations in religion juice, but at least we have conversations, which is way better than nothing. If her love for me has to go through Jesus, then Christ can lubricate us.

I see her once a month, under heavily guarded supervision, psychiatric observation, and handcuffs on my wrist. It's not too bad, she's allowed to stroke my hands. We like hand stroking, Mama and I.

She learns big chunks of the Bible off by heart and recites them to me like lullabies. That book is full of love, murder, rape, war, torture, terrorism, and cataclysms. With its incredible journeys, its monsters, and its magic, it's pretty good stuff. They should make it into a movie or a TV show. It was written over centuries, with a shit ton of collaborators, professional authors, the best of the time. It's well-made and well-documented, everything's in there. From now on, I'm a one-book kinda guy.

I have everything I need: a roof, three meals a day, excellent subsidized drugs, and a united family. Anything beyond that is just a luxury unattainable by someone as disadvantaged as me.

I'm well-known. My mother loves me. Never again will I need to kill or write. Never.

I've survived destiny and conquered death. Now all I have to do is kill some time.

AUTHOR'S ACKNOWLEDGEMENTS

Thank you to Hazel Millar and Jay MillAr; you do exceptional work for both Canadian and Quebec literature. It is an honour to be published by your press.

Thank you to J. C. Sutcliffe, for your patience, your kindness, and the quality of your translations. I knew Mama's Boy would be in good hands with you.

Marie-Eve Gélinas, thank you for this beautiful love story of literature. Even in my craziest dreams I could never have imagined a better editor.

The entire team at Groupe Librex, thank you for breathing life into the Beast. I am indebted to you. Please always stay so wonderfully passionate; it's rare and luminous.

Thank you to all readers open-minded enough to allow the Beast in; to all readers perceptive enough to savour the second and third degrees of meaning; to booksellers honest enough to suggest different and disturbing books.

The Beast, you Mama's Boy, my brother, my muse, my utterly unacceptable character, I will miss you. Thank you for these three wild rides. It's well-documented…

TRANSLATOR'S ACKNOWLEDGEMENTS

Thank you to Jay and Hazel for their ongoing support and all the excellent work they do at Book*hug, and thanks to David for the fun wordplay and the crazy journey.

ABOUT THE AUTHOR

Jocelyn Riendeau

DAVID GOUDREAULT is a Québécois novelist, poet, columnist, and social worker. He is the author of the bestselling La Bête trilogy, which includes *La Bête à sa mère* (*Mama's Boy*, Book*hug, 2018), *La Bête et sa cage* (*Mama's Boy Behind Bars*, Book*hug, 2019), and *Abattre la bête* (*Mama's Boy: Game Over*, Book*hug, 2020). He has also published three poetry collections. His latest novel is *Ta mort à moi*. He was the first person from Quebec to win the Poetry World Cup in Paris (2011), and he has also received many other awards, including the Médaille de l'Assemblée Nationale (2012), the Prix des Nouvelles Voix de la Littérature (2016), the Prix de la ville de Sherbrooke (2016), the Grand Prix Littéraire Archambault (2016), and the Prix Lèvres Urbaines (2017). His work has been published internationally in France and Mexico. Goudreault lives in Sherbrooke, Quebec.

ABOUT THE TRANSLATOR

J.C. SUTCLIFFE is a writer, translator, and editor who has lived in England, France, and Canada. She has reviewed books for the *Times Literary Supplement*, *The Globe and Mail*, and the *National Post*, among others. Her recent translations include *Mama's Boy* and *Mama's Boy Behind Bars* by David Goudreault, *Document 1* by François Blais, and *Worst Case, We Get Married* by Sophie Bienvenu.

COLOPHON

Manufactured as the first English edition of
Mama's Boy Game Over
in the fall of 2020 by Book*hug Press.

Type + design by Tree Abraham
Copy edited by Stuart Ross

bookhugpress.ca

Don't miss the first two books in
David Goudreault's Mama's Boy trilogy,
available from Book*hug Press

Mama's Boy

$20

ISBN 9781771663823

Written with gritty humour in the form
of a confession, *Mama's Boy* recounts
the family drama of a young man who
sets out in search of his mother after a
childhood spent shuffling from one
foster home to another. A bizarre
character with a skewed view of the
world, he leads the reader on a quest
that is both tender and violent.

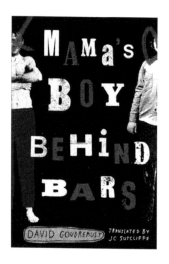

Mama's Boy Behind Bars

$20

ISBN 9781771664851

Mama's Boy finds himself in jail
following a search for his long lost
mother. There, he sets out to make
a name for himself and achieve his
ambition of joining the ranks of
hardcore criminals. But things get
wildly complicated when he falls in
love with a prison guard. Can
Mama's Boy juggle love and crime?